RUN,
REBEL

RUN
REBEL

Manjeet Mann

PENGUIN BOOKS

PENGUIN BOOKS

UK | USA | Canada | Ireland | Australia
India | New Zealand | South Africa

Penguin Books is part of the Penguin Random House group of companies
whose addresses can be found at global.penguinrandomhouse.com.

www.penguin.co.uk
www.puffin.co.uk
www.ladybird.co.uk

First published 2020

001

Text copyright © Manjeet Mann, 2020

The moral right of the author has been asserted

Text design by Janene Spencer
Printed and bound in Great Britain by Clays Ltd, Elcograf S.p.A.

A CIP catalogue record for this book is available from the British Library

ISBN: 978–0–241–41142–1

All correspondence to:
Penguin Books
Penguin Random House Children's
80 Strand, London WC2R 0RL

Penguin Random House is committed to a
sustainable future for our business, our readers
and our planet. This book is made from Forest
Stewardship Council® certified paper.

For

Joe

and

all the women and girls who dare to rebel

PROLOGUE

A wound.
Triggered
by a beating.

It grew.
Thriving
on neglect.

It swelled.
Flourishing
on her spine.

When ripe,
a clotted
blister.

It.
Crippled.
Her.

Weighing down
on her
too-small

frame
for her
adolescent age.

My. Mother.
Sat
hunchback,

working.

Silent.

Ignored and ignoring
pins of
prickly pain pulsing.

What's wrong with your daughter?
a neighbour asked.

*She's not
sitting or standing upright?
It's been weeks.*

My grandmother
looked at
my mother

as if she were
observing her
for the first time.

My grandmother

fell
to
the
floor.

*Crumpled like a sheet
falling from
a washing line,*
my mother tells me.

Slumped
on the back
of a motorbike,

my mother travelled
along dusty dirt tracks,
through several Indian villages

to the nearest hospital.
The poison
drained.

The rotten flesh
carved,
           gouged,
                   burrowed
                            out.

My mother
concealed her
anger.

Her mother
showed no
remorse.

The wound –
now
a scar.

The size
of a fist.

A crater
buried between
shoulder blades.

It is the curse of being a girl,
my mother tells me.

You are the property of your
parents, husband, brothers.
You endure,
never question it.

I question it.

ONE
RESTLESSNESS

ANATOMY OF
A REVOLUTION
STAGE 1

People feel restless.
Held down by
restrictions,
forced to
accept
less.

Preparing to fight,
accepting all
they will
lose.

BOUND

Built-in fear
of our families,
the community,
we are **O**bserved
thro**U**gh the gaze of others.
Socialized into tracking each other.
Friends, neighbours, family.

Is she where she should be?
Should she be out this late?
Who is that she's walking with?

Watching.
Mo**N**itoring

and **d**ying to get out.

I AM 1

Bewakoof.
The Punjabi word for
stupid.

I.
Am.
Stupid.

Nikame.
The Punjabi word for
useless.

I.
Am.
Useless.

My name is
Amber Rai.

Amber.
The stone of
courage.

The soul
of a
tiger.

Rai,
from the Sanskrit *raja*.
A title of honour.

A leader.
A king.
A chief.

But
at home

I am
stupid
and
I am
useless.

BURDEN

No one wanted my mother.
No one wanted her mother,
and no one wanted her mother.

It goes on and on
now and
way back then.

No one wanted Ruby.
No one wanted me.

My sister Ruby and I
have heard
the stories.

The sadness that
cloaked
our births.

The prayers
and temple visits,
wishing,

wishing
we would come out
as boys.

So we are born
in all our
feminine form

and reminded
of our
burden

every day.

We are obedient.
We are small.
We are quiet.

To prove
we are
not

a burden.

We are still reminded
that we are a
burden.

It   eats   away   at   you.

CONFUSED

If girls are never wanted,
how do you expect
to get

your
precious
little
boy?

MY VOICE

No matter how small or quiet I am expected to be,
I find my voice on the running track. It's where I'm truly alive.

Words boomerang from trainer to tarmac. Creating
ripples in every corner of my body until all

knock-downs, run-ins, face-offs and scraps
have been   twisted   wrung   exhausted

                                                up

                        up

and released   up
into the clouds and sky above.

DREAMS

So simple. To run.
A professional athlete.
It's a stupid dream.

Ruby's dreams were crushed.
She was overpowered, tamed.
She chose not to fight.

Mum must have had dreams.
She's never spoken of them.
Must be too painful.

Dad sleep-talks his dreams.
They keep us awake at night.
Dreams trapped in nightmares.

PREDICTION

Home
is not
where my
heart is.

Freedom
usually comes
at a
price.

I am restless,
my feet
need to fly.

It's only
a matter
of time.

Correction.

I *fear*
it's only
a matter

of

time.

FIRST DAY BACK

I leave for school earlier than usual.
Meeting with Tara and David at our secret place.

My stomach doing flips holding in – excitement.
Not seeing them over the summer makes holidays – unbearable.

Correction.

Not seeing David over the summer makes holidays
HELL ON EARTH.

I turn out of my estate, take in the tree-lined street that surrounds
me and leave the looming high-rises behind.

THE ESTATE

Palm Wood Estate
is one of the roughest
and biggest estates
in the country.

Streets in the sky dreams
turned to
sinkhole nightmares.

THE GRASS IS GREENER

I stride past
the bookies,
the chippy,
the newsagent's.

Get to our secret place – quicker.
See Tara and David – sooner.

Turn on to streets that
enjoy sky and
green spaces.
Breathe air that

suggests it's cleaner,
pass houses that promise
better futures and
shops that

promise healthier
hearts and minds,
as the eyes of the
high-rises
       fade

          into

            the

              distance.

OUR SECRET PLACE

St Martin's Church
dominates the skyline.
A thing of beauty
in a place that
has been 'voted'

Britain's

worst town.
Unhealthiest town.
Grimmest town.
And – the latest –
most deprived town.

An unfair review
of a town that's
split in two.
St Martin's stands
at the divide

between council tenants
and homeowners.
Between the unemployed
and the employed.

A divided town
where prosperity
and poverty
are neighbours.
A postcode lottery
cementing futures.

At St Martin's
none of that matters.
It's neutral, it's beautiful,
it's safe.

A ROOM WITH A VIEW

If I stand on the toilet in our house and look out of the bathroom window,
I can see it.

Ruby and I would rush to tiptoe-peek out of the window
when the church bells rang on a Sunday morning.

In religious studies we were told the spiritual weight of a church bell
could drive away 'evil spirits' and storms.

Hypnotized by the melodic chimes, we stood transfixed.
Our toes numbing on the cold plastic rim as

we prayed the bells would drive away the tempest
that engulfed our own home.

SECRET CORNERS

St Martin's has many hidden places
concealed by oversized gravestones.

I head towards our secluded corner, screened in
on *three* sides and camouflaged by a giant oak.

I can hear their voices. I poke my head round.
Tara squeals and jumps up and down.

AmberAmberAmber!

She grabs me and gives me
the biggest squeeze ever.

I've missed your beautiful face!

Tara is the only person who calls me beautiful.
I try and believe it.

David holds out his arms.

**Sister from another mister,
come here!**

He gives me an almighty hug, which makes my
heart do a little flip.

Bro-ther   f-rom   a-n-oth-er   mo-th-er!

I can barely get the words out, David's embrace is so tight.
He smells of strawberry chewing gum and Lynx.

I take a moment to try and breathe him in
and sink into his shoulder.

Being with these two grounds me
like the giant oak that shields us.

I feel rooted and protected as he
stands in front of me, his hands still on my arms,

grinning, chewing and smelling great.
He looks different. Slightly more tanned,

streaks of blond in his dark hair.
His eyes wider, his lashes longer.

He looks way hotter than I remember him six weeks ago.
Waaaaaay hotter. I didn't think that was even possible.

Hot,
I say.

Not in my head but out **loud.**

What?

Tara, staring at me, staring at David
for   way   too   long.

Hmmm?
Nothing.
I'm just hot.
Are you hot?
I'm really hot.

ACT COOL

Tara and David talk
excitedly about
their summer holiday.

Their lips
bouncing words
back and forth,

finishing each other's
sentences.
I barely get a word in.

I bought you something!

Tara starts rummaging in her bag.
She gives me a beautiful box
with pastel flowers painted on all sides.

Her eyes sparkling,
her mouth all smiles
and cherry lipgloss.

I open the box and
give the contents a sniff.

It's a sage candle.
It'll help cleanse any negative energy
by balancing out your emotions.
You should light it when you meditate.

David and I share a look.
It's not to be unkind.
It's just that this is *so*
Tara.

I saw that look!
It works, OK! Trust me.
My mum cleanses the energy in our house
with a sage stick every week.

It's great, honestly. Thank you.

Any-waaay! Tara rolls her eyes.
It really was THE BEST holiday, Amber!

I'm trying my best
to look neutral,
not resentful.

It was a last-minute deal.
My mum just booked it.

David,
trying to act –
a little cooler.

He leans in	closer,
his mouth	at my ear,
his breath	hot
as he pulls me in	tighter.

It wasn't a big deal. Honestly.

His arm	round my waist –
it feels	*glorious.*

I try and act cool,
　　　　. . . but I can't help wonder . . .
try not to
　　　　. . . is he . . .
draw attention to
　　　　. . . flirting?
the blood
　　　　. . . no . . .
rushing to
　　　　. . . never . . .
my cheeks.
　　　　. . . impossible.

. . . And then we were like,
ahhh, we're going on holiday!

Tara unable to act –
cooler.

I do my best
fake smile,
fake happy voice.

Wow, must have been so much fun.

The weather was amazing!
We went DIVING, Amber! DIVING!
It was sooooo cool!

That sounds amazing.

My mouth doing all sorts of lying,
saying the opposite
of what my heart's feeling.

We missed you.
Wished you were there.

The way he looks at me . . .
it's like he's saying,
I missed you,
I wished you were there.

David moves his arm
up from my waist
to round my neck,
resting his head on my shoulder.

Fake smiles
and fake voices
don't fool him.

He gives me a wink.
Which makes my stomach
do another flip.

I tell myself I'm imagining it all.
He would never like me,
not like that –
ever.

Here we are,
going on and on.
How was your summer break?

OPTIONS

Option 1: Lie.
Option 2: Tell the truth.

CONCEAL 1

Fine. Nothing to report. So boring!

I don't believe that for a second.

Believe it. It's true.

Come on, something cool must have happened?

Ummmmmmm, nope, not really.

Something traumatic?
Yes.
Cool?

NO.

CONCEAL 2

Keeping silent about all
the bits that make
you up creates
a lot of noise
in your
head.

CONCEAL 3

Despite these two being my best friends,
I am unable to fully commit to
option 2.

They don't know
where my mum works.
(Their mums have really good jobs.)

They don't know my dad
doesn't work.
(Their dads have really good jobs.)

They don't know we rely
on benefits.
(Don't want the label *benefit scum*.)

They don't know I rely on
second-hand clothes.
(They have all the latest gear.)

They've never been to my house,
although they know where I live.
(They live in the nicer part of town.)

I told them about Ruby,
how we are no longer the sisters we used to be.
(Because that was too painful to keep inside.)

They know about *The Man*
who lives opposite me.
(Because I was too frightened.)

I don't tell them about
what goes on in my house.
(Because some things are best kept secret.)

CONCEAL 4

Nothing
is as
lonely
as a

secret.

DAVID

Caramel skin,
hazel eyes,
thick wavy dark hair.

Correction.
Thick wavy dark hair
with streaks
of blond.

Average height,
athletic build,
great smile.

Correction.
Gorgeous smile.
A swoon-worthy smile.
A smile that has
the power to leave me
in a giddy mess for days.

I've liked him
since day one,
Year Seven.

I'd never seen
eyes
hair
eyes
mouth
cheekbones
face
mouth
eyes
cheekbones
eyes
mouth
mouth
mouth
mouth

like his before.

JUST FRIENDS

He sat behind me in regiStration in the corner by
the window, and if the sun was shining just right
I could catch his rEflection in the glass.

Tara says he's got a quiet Confidence. He's not
like other boys. He's quiet, sensitive, self-assured
without the arRogance. When Tara's

sanitary towel fell out of her bag and all the boys
in the class thrEw it round the room like a frisbee,
David snatched it out of Paul's hand, gave iT

back to Tara and told everyone to grow up. That's
when we started hanging out and we've been
inseparable ever since. I was over the moon when he

joined athletics Club. Two evenings a week. Just us.
And yet we remain JUST fRiends. Strictly school
friends. Apart from athletics we NEVER hang

oUt after school. In school, I'm his sister from
another mister and he'S my brother from another
mother and it

hurts.

TARA

Petite and curvy.
Long wavy red hair
down to her lower back.
The brightest, bluest eyes
you will ever see.

Ocean blue.

Walking with Tara
always results in boys
doing double takes,
drowning in her good looks.

Tara is kind, quirky
with a big heart.
It was just the two of us
until David joined.

It's not quantity,
it's quality.

That's what she always says.
Not the *number* of friends
but the *type* of friend.

Tara is always coming
out with gems like that.

Tara refers to my anger as
passion.

You just feel things really deeply is all.

She says it with an arm
round my shoulder,
trying to soften the truth.

Her mum is an 'alternative therapist'
and Tara's always telling me to meditate.

It'll help when you feel yourself getting worked up, she says.
Or give up gluten!
Food allergies can make us freak out.

They say three's a crowd,
but not with us.

I AM 2

Lanky
long-faced
some say
hard-faced.

Dark
small eyes
some say
mean eyes.

Warm
try to be
some say
ice-cold.

SCHOOL

Supposed to inspire
the next

generation.

Concrete blocks
and shipping containers

do nothing but
motivate you to

swim away.

Classes so big
they give teachers

breakdowns

because they've been

let down.

Just like the kids.
Not many go on to do anything

special.

Some defy the norm, breaking

free.

Giving us all hope we can

soar.

This year will I fly or will I F
A
L
L?

GIRLS, GIRLS, GIRLS

I notice them   giggling.

Looking in David's   direction.

Looking at each other   whispering.

Accidentally on purpose   pushing

                                       into him.

COOL GIRL 1

Tara gets knocked into a wall
as cool girl Cora
steps in front
of us.

Love the highlights, David.

Cool girl Cora
runs her fingers
through
David's
hair.

It's natural actually. Just happens in the sun,
he stutters.

You're SO adorable!
she says and struts down the hall,
all perfume and hitched-up
skirt like she's on a
catwalk.

Tara rubs her arm, trying not
to be bothered by
cool girl Cora.

Such weird energy today, she says.
I knew I should've brought my crystals with me.

NEW HOME

We head to registration,
the three of us together.

New school year,
new class,
new rules.

We scan the room.
We consider where
best to place ourselves.

These will be our seats
for the rest of the year –
not a decision to be taken lightly.

The *cool* girls and boys sit at the back.
The *loners* sit in the corners.
The *swots* at the front.

That leaves
the middle row.
Our new home
for the rest of the year.

COOL GIRL 2

A ball of paper strikes the back
of David's head.

Oops, sorry!
I just wanted to say hi.

Cool girl Bryony sits leaning over her desk,
all blusher and fake eyelashes.

Looks like everyone's noticed David's hotness
has gone up over the summer.

Er, hi.

David's cheeks flush
with embarrassment.

Did you have a good summer?

Her smile wide,
her eyes fluttering.

Er, yeah.

He turns and sits down.

Bryony, surprised by the abrupt ending
to the conversation,

starts whispering, all flustered, with
the other cool girls.

David starts taking books out of his bag,
cheeks still red.

I look at Tara.

Tara looks at me.

It seems we are *both* equally troubled
by this exchange.

FAKING IT

I nudge David in the ribs.

Ooh, did you have a nice summer?
Ooh, hi, David.
Sorry, just wanted to get your
ATTENTION.

OOH, DAVID, I LURVVVVE YOU.

Oi, shut up!

You better not ditch us for the cool gang.

As if!
Plus, they are so far from cool.
We're the actual cool ones.
They're just sheep,
WE are the shepherds!

Yeah, right!

I agree with David and, if you don't believe it,
just fake it till you make it!

We all hold
our heads a little
higher
our backs a little
straighter
as we march
to our first lesson
of the year.

TRUTH

English class
with Mr Walker.

He talks about truth.

It's where all good stories come from.
We'll be focusing on autobiographical writing this term.
Write your truth.

He gives me an extra long
icy stare.
Raising his eyebrows
like he's expecting me
to disappoint him.

Mr Walker has told me
on more than one occasion
that I lack creative flair.
He had high hopes
for me.
He taught Ruby.
Ruby was his

star pupil.

But

words don't flow
from my brain
on to the page.

Fear builds
an Everest of walls
in my head.

I look round the class.
No one can know my truth.

A pact made before
I could speak,
silenced before
my first words.

The secrets I keep,
the fears I carry
must remain
behind the closed doors
of the home
they were birthed in.

Once again,
like most people
from estates like mine,
it feels as though I've lost
before I've even started.

THE GAME OF SHAME

In geography,
permission slips
for field trips
for my parents to sign.

Correction.

For me to sign.

Pretending to be a parent.
Pretending they can sign their name.
Pretending they can read.
Pretending to hide their shame.

Correction.

My shame.

MR HISTORY JONES

Before I started secondary school
Ruby gave me the low-down
on every teacher.

The nice ones
the weird ones
the strict ones
the inspiring ones
the boring ones.

The classes you can mess around in and
the classes where you can't.

Mr Geography Jones, she said,
is one of the boring ones.
She doesn't know why he teaches,
he clearly has no passion for it.

Mr History Jones on the other hand
is one of the inspiring ones.
He bounds round the classroom
like an excited puppy.

She insisted he'd make me love history.
He won't.
No one has
in the last five years.

Learning about king blah-blah
back in the whatever century
bores me to death.

Even with Mr History Jones
and his one-man re-enactments
of Henry VIII and all his wives.

I fail to see what makes it relevant,
how any of it relates to the present
and how any of it relates to me.

HISTORY SYLLABUS

My eyelids are already feeling heavy
as I yawn through
the syllabus for the year.

The French revolution of   1789.
The European revolutions of   1848.
The Russian revolution of   1917.

There are two books we need.

The Anatomy of the European Revolutions 1848–1917
by Robert Elderidge.

And

The Art of Revolution
by Mary S. Pierce.

There are a few copies we can borrow.
My eyes fix on the small pile on his desk.

No iPhone, iPad, laptop, iMac.
Nothing worse than spending every lunchtime

on the school computer and there's no way
I'm asking Mum for money to buy study aids.

I just can't do it, she said the last time I asked.
Do you want to eat or do you want books?

Mr History Jones begins writing on the board
as sheets of paper are passed round the class.

The handout lands on my desk.
The words sing off the page.

A revolution.
The forcible overthrow of a government
or social order in favour of a new regime.

The anatomy of a revolution, he calls it,
and there are eight stages.

He scribbles them on the board,
simplifying each stage in one word.

We are to elaborate on each stage for homework,
prompting a collective groan

to break out around the class
just as the bell rings for lunch.

THE ANATOMY OF A REVOLUTION

One	Restlessness
Two	Dissatisfaction
Three	Control
Four	Momentum
Five	Honeymoon
Six	Terror
Seven	Overthrow
Eight	Peace

ONE WORD

It leaps out
over and over
as I read

down

the

page.

Overthrow

Overthrow

> **Overthrow**

Overthrow

Overthrow.

Something stirs inside,
makes me feel
like I have
superpowers.

I continue scanning
the stages and
my eyes fix
on another word.

One word that
flips
superpower
to powerless.

Terror.

Terror.

TERROR.

WHISPERS

There is a queue
for the books
at the end
of class.

I get the last copy
of each one
and stuff them
into my bag.

I walk out into the hall.

Revolution . . .

Feeling the weight of
the books on my shoulders.

The forcible overthrow . . .

I can't help but feel.

A new regime . . .

They are whispering to me.

SHEEP

Me, Tara and David
sit sharing a family-sized bag of crisps.
I'm convinced he's sitting
a little closer to Tara,
closer than he used to,
as we watch the cool girls
talking to the cool boys
in the middle of the schoolyard.

We roll our eyes
every time they scream
when a football
comes hurtling
towards them.

We laugh as they
all try to duck
and shield themselves
from getting whacked
on the head,

and the cool boys
puff out their chests
and stick their middle fingers up
at the boys playing football.

The cool girls giggle,
flick their hair
and hitch up
their skirts
a little higher.

The school bell rings
and we crease up
with laughter when
David bleats like a sheep
in their direction.

DOUBLE PE

Straight after lunch,
with my kit bag
swung over my shoulder,
I head towards the minibus
taking us to King Edward's sports field.

The private school that has it all.
Not a shipping container in sight.
It's all tennis courts,
football pitches
and athletics track.

It's the school we all wish
we could drop our anchor in
and be given a chance to thrive
in ways we never knew we could. ·

MINIBUS POLITICS 1

Cool girls at the back.
Everyone else,
anywhere else.

RUNNING

School field.
Muddy, damp, cold.
I love it.
I'm on my own,
I get transported,
I feel free.
It's the only time
I ever really feel FREE.

Team sports don't appeal.
Hockey at our school is like
gang warfare.
An hour of getting battered and bruised,
girls coming at me with sticks –
aiming for ankles.
But the running track . . .

Now . . .

The track is my time.

I shift my thoughts,
try and
make sense of . . .
stuff.

With each stride
I zoom through anger,
leap through sadness,
tear through loneliness

and

come out
the other side
newer, happier, better.

ALWAYS better
than before.

It feels like
the world
slows down.

Allowing me
to catch up
with thoughts
that usually race.

I go to places in my head
that aren't here,
of this place,
of this time.

The lines in my head
get tangled, see.

They criss-cross,
get mixed up.

Running makes the lines
s t r a i g h t e r.

Turns down the rage
in my stomach.

Loosens the phantom grip
on my throat.

Provides respite
from the familiar
urge to
escape.

Running
gives me a purpose.

Running
gives me a reason
                    to live.

ON THE STARTING BLOCK

On your marks.

Focus.

Get ready!

Inhale.

Set.

Exhale.

Go.

Run.

TWO HUNDRED METRES

Legs rotating,
trainers striking
tarmac beneath
my feet.

Quick breaths,
sharp looks

to my left,
Sarah,
behind
for now.

To my right,
Leanne,
neck
and neck.

Heart pumping,
legs pounding,
arms propelling.

Flashes of last night.
The crying.
I stumble.

Smashed plates.
The blood.
Lines blur.

I weave
in and out
of lanes.

Almost trip
on Leanne's ankle,

allow Sarah
an advantage

as she closes
the gap between us.

Stay in your lane, Amber!

Miss Sutton's voice
snaps me back
to the present.

Go, Amber!

Tara shouting
from the sideline,
jumping up and down,
fist pumping the air.

Just the spark I need.

I charge myself up.
Waves of electricity
firing through

arms   legs   heart   veins.

As I cross the finish line

FIRST.

I catch my breath,
high-five
Leanne and Sarah.

Fantastic times, girls.
All three of you impressive.
Especially you, Amber.

Thanks, Miss.

Have you been training over the summer?

No, Miss. I wish.

She raises her eyebrows.
Nods, like she's impressed
I've still got it
and haven't turned
into some slug
over the summer break.

No time for hanging around.
Two laps of the field.
Go!

Sarah and Leanne aren't having it.
Pleading with Miss Sutton:

Need to lie down after that
two-hundred-metre sprint, Miss!

I leave the groans behind.
Start lapping up the laps,
wishing I could do this forever.

'**IT**'

Runner's high.

It's
euphoria.

A cloud-nine
dreamland
that can last
for days.

Non-
stop.

Those days are
rare.

Mostly
it
sticks around

on the track
in the shower
in the changing room.

That's about it
for *it*.
That's usually
as long as *it* lasts.

When the school bell rings,
I start to sink
as *it* floats away.

Drowning as I
freestyle panic-crawl
to my estate.

Sometimes
it lingers.

Just long enough
to coax me through the front door
and swift-sprint me to
the sanctuary of my room.

It aids my invisibility.
Allows me to disappear
from the eruption of
household demands
spewing from
beer-stench breath.

PRIVILEGE

I wanted to avoid this conversation
with Miss Sutton.
I wanted to avoid
having to
explain,
lie
and

make excuses.

No such luck.

*Your time has improved. Keep that up and it's enough to get us to the
finals of the ESAC. You have a chance of being picked for the under-
seventeen British team. I've looked at last year's winning times for the
two-hundred metre track and you could beat it, Amber. Do you hear
what I'm saying? Don't let last year's disappointment hold you back.*

I can't compete this year, Miss.

Why? You're our star runner!

I shrug.
Look down.
Kick my heels
into grass.

*You've got a shot at being on the British team, to compete
internationally.
Do you know what that could mean for your future?
Don't you want that?*

I shrug, thinking I should
have run slower.

Thinking about how much
I didn't want to have
this conversation.

It's not up to me.

I wouldn't be doing my job if I didn't encourage my best student to fulfil her potential.

I can't, Miss. My dad said after last year's championships that was it.

What about your mum?

She . . . she tried. But it's no good.

I'm sorry, Amber, I'm having trouble understanding.

Of course she is.
Because, in Miss Sutton's
privileged world,
we exist on the same
level playing field.

It's just his way, Miss.

There's only one other athlete I've taught who's shown the same talent as you. You know who I'm talking about . . .

Yes, Miss. Sorry, Miss.

I glance up momentarily.
She looks all hopeful,
like comparing me to Allie Reid
is all it'll take
to reverse decisions
that are out of my control.

I don't know what to say. I'm so surprised, I wasn't expecting this at all.

That's the problem with privilege.
If you have it,
it can be hard to imagine
why others can't live as freely as you.

Like I said, not up to me, Miss.

But I thought you wanted to be a professional athlete.
What happened to that dream? This could help get you there.

I catch a fleeting look of frustration
sweeping across her face.

That's the problem with privilege.
If you have it,
the world is your oyster.
Become, do and have
whatever you please.

I keep looking down.
I kick my heels
into grass.
Notice the sole
of my left trainer
breaking free
from the toe.

Flapping like a
giant mouth
doing the talking
I can't.

I try and hide it,
kicking toe into grass,
but I'm too late.

Sign of a great athlete. A well-worn trainer. We might have
some in lost property if that helps.

No, it's fine. My mum's buying me new ones.

Both our cheeks
flush red.
I don't know
which of us
is more embarrassed.

I'll write a letter to your parents explaining why we need you
on the team.

I'm so disappointed
by the lameness
of this idea.

I don't think that will help, Miss.

The county team managers had their eye on you last year.
They all said you had great promise. We can't give up!

That's the thing about privilege.
Those that have it
never fear resistance.

THE ESAC

The English Schools' Athletics Championships.

One of the largest athletics events
in the world.

Nearly all Olympic athletes
have come up through this route.

County team managers scout for the most
promising athletes during the competition.

It is up to them who goes through to the next round.

First you compete in the inter-school games –
the best athletes make it to regional finals.

If you win at regionals you are chosen to
compete at county level and the

honour of being best in the country
in your chosen sport.

Miss Sutton first mentioned it
in Year Eight, after sports day.

I won the school medal for the
one AND two hundred metres.

That's when she told me about
Allie Reid.

ALLIE REID

Olympic athlete.
One and two hundred
metres track.

She won gold in the
Commonwealth Games,
the World Championships

and
she's competed
in the Olympics.

Also,
we share
the same initials.

A. R.
Amber Rai.
Allie Reid.

Miss Sutton coached her.
Said she sees
the same spark

in me
that she saw
in her.

We both
come ALIVE
on the track.

DAD'S WORDS

You're not a little girl any more.
You're fifteen, nearly sixteen.
You are a woman.
Women don't run round fields
in little shorts
for the world to stare at.
We allowed you too much freedom.
It ends.
Now.

And when Mum
took my side
he slapped her so hard
she had a bruise for two weeks.

There's no dream
worth fighting for
if it results in that.

I said, **Sorry.**
She said, It wasn't your fault.

But it was,
is,
so now

the dreaming stops.

NEXT TIME...

I missed out on a medal
at last year's
county championships.

Everyone said it was
bad luck and so close.
They said,
Next time, it'll be your turn.

I guess I'll never know.

SELFIES

Tara has her phone out and
takes loads of photos
on the minibus back to school.
Tara teaching me the right angle
for the perfect portrait.

The phone needs to be –
up high.
Our chins need to be –
down.
Our faces need to be –
turned to the left.
It elongates your face,
brings out your cheekbones –
apparently.

(Sometimes it helps
if you look away.
Like you've just seen something
in the distance
and the phone
just happened
to take a photo of you.)

Look up.
Slight pout –
not too much.
Don't want to *look* like you're pouting.
Don't want to *look* like you've set up the shot.
Got to look *natural*.

Although
there's nothing natural
about these photos.
They are posed to perfection.

Now silly ones.
Suck our cheekbones in.
Cross our eyes.
Stick out our tongues.

Tara looks great.
Even in the silly photos
she still manages to pose
just right.

This one's great!
I'll send it to David, she says.

No, don't, I look horrible.

Why do you care? It's just David.

Because . . . please just don't.

What's the big deal?
He'll think it's funny.

I know but . . .

Ooops, too late!

Tara!

I want to scream.
Tara's laughing,
telling me
not to be so serious.

I stare out of the window.
Try and ignore
Tara sending David
every one of the photos
we've just taken.

Can't get too angry,
can't make it obvious,
can't let on that
over the summer holidays
I missed him
and any feelings I had before
have quadrupled in size,

and I can't tell Tara
that lately
I find myself wondering
where he is and
what he's doing
more than I used to,
more than I should.
More like

all. The. **Time.**

EYES TALK

Tara talks
non-stop about her
summer holiday.

Her summer holiday
with David.

I want to *know* everything
but at the same time
I don't want to *hear* any of it.

I keep thinking about the fact
that he's seen her in a bikini.

Tara scrolls through her phone,
showing me pictures of the holiday.

I take in every photo
of the two of them
together.

Analysing
how close they might be sitting,
if their hands are touching,
if they have their arms round each other,
but most of all
what their *eyes* are saying.

Tara talks about
eyes being the window
to a person's soul.

Smiling eyes
sad eyes
dishonest eyes
pupils getting bigger
when you fancy someone.

I'm trying to look at their eyes.

Tara's putting new filters
on old photos.
Cropping and changing,
brightening and lightening.

Till they look
unreal.

And she's saying things like,
Isn't it weird how we spent every day together,
and didn't get sick of each other!

And,
Oh my God! That was taken just before
a bird pooped on David's shoulder!
It was SO funny!

I smile
and laugh,
act cool,

but all I want to do
is take her phone
and zoom in on their pupils.

Especially in the photo
where they're looking at each other,
drinking from straws
out of the *same* coconut.

They are my friends.
My best friends.
I don't want to be feeling
all these *things*

but

I've noticed that they're
both acting a little different.

I can't ask them.
I don't want confirmation.
(It's better *not* knowing.)

But, at the same time, I do!

My brain feels like it's going to
explode.

THOUGHTS

What did you do every day?

Did you kiss?

Are you in love?

Is three a crowd?

Did you talk about me?

Three's a crowd, right?

If you did talk about me, what did you say?

Do you still want to be mates?

Do you want me out of the group?

He can't love you. He can't.

He can love you. He can.

Look at her, she's beautiful. There's no contest.

She's your friend. Stop thinking of it as a contest.

You don't own him. He's not yours.

Why am I bothered? I'm not allowed to date – anyone.

STOP!!

Bury this.

Bury this like I bury everything else.

GREEN-EYED MONSTER 1

I'm trying to keep down
the eruption of thoughts
overflowing in my mind
but one escapes, and before
I have a chance to swallow
it spews out.

**So when you got back from Cyprus
did you both still hang out?**

Yeah, a bit, I mean, not lots.

I want to ask,
How much is A BIT?
What do you mean, NOT LOTS?
Every week?
Every day?
Every other day?
What is the measure of time between
A BIT and NOT LOTS?!

Are you OK? You seem really pissed off?

I'm fine!
I snap.
I mean, I'm fine,
I say, softening
the snap.

You should definitely light that sage candle tonight.

She turns her body towards mine,
reaches across and
puts her hands on my shoulders,
her eyes closed.

What are you doing?!

Shhhh, I'm doing 'hands-on healing'.

I don't need healing, Tara!

I try to shrug her hands off my shoulders.

Shhhh. Everyone needs healing, Amber.

GEMMA

Someone starts singing
some annoying pop song.

One voice carries over the rest.
One voice that grates.

I turn to see her braiding her hair.
Our eyes catch for a moment.

Gemma. Griffin.

DON'T BE FOOLED

Gemma Griffin
thinks she's all that.

Rich mum and dad,
little Miss Perfect.

Yeah, she thinks she's all that.

Acts all shy,
victim-like –
couldn't be
further from the truth.
She gives as good as she gets,
and that's a fact.

Yeah, she thinks she's all that.

I know what she's thinking,
looking down on me.
I see her,
she doesn't need to say it,
I can just tell.

'I wouldn't say a bad word about anyone' *eyes*
'I'm so innocent' *face*
'I'm minding my own business' *HAIR*
I see it.

Yeah, she thinks she's all that.

Looks at me
like I'm . . .
like I'm . . .

Nothing.

Yeah, she thinks she's all THAT.

HANGING BACK

I take my time getting off the minibus.
Tara's telling me to get a move on.

In a minute!
I shout back.

I look through the minibus window.
What's taking her so long?
I see her tying her shoelace.
I can see she sees me.
Taking her time,
hoping I'll lose interest.

Not likely.

My mind wanders.
I see David waiting
at the school gates,
Tara approaching.
My jaw tightens
as I stare,
watching them
playfully nudge each other.

A momentary lapse,
forget I'm watching,
waiting
for Gemma.
Don't notice her leg it off the bus
and run out of the school gates
till it's too late.

You can run but you can't hide!
I shout.

A group of Year Sevens
turn round.

What you lot looking at?

They turn,
quicken their pace
as I start walking.

Next time,
I think.

Next time.

Run towards Tara and David,
join in with them
and their *playful* game of nudge.

A RISK

After school
we walk down Church Hill.
Me, Tara
and David.

This is a risk
but I'm not ready
to say goodbye,

not ready to
let go of David
for the day.

I'll be safe in Mackie D's
where I can find excuses to:

sit close
look into his eyes
watch his mouth
make him laugh
touch the top of his arm
put my head on his shoulder
twirl my hair
memorize his scent –

keep an eye on Tara.

AUNTIES

I tell David to walk ahead,
not with us,
tell him
we'll meet up in Mackie D's.

But him and Tara keep talking.
He's all excited about athletics club,
thinking he's gonna be
the next Mo Farah.

My mind's elsewhere.
Concentrating on not being seen.
Looking out for familiar faces,
avoiding well-known places
where aunties and uncles
might work or shop.

It's rush hour.

Cars taking over
the quiet backstreets.
I look at the pavement,
hide my face as we walk.

Traffic lights.

We stop.
Waiting –
for that green spot
to turn to red.

David, don't stand next to me.

Where else am I supposed to stand?

Not next to me!

He rolls his eyes.
He doesn't move.

Cars passing by.
I hide behind Tara,
use her as a sort of –
barrier.

Traffic stops.

I cross quickly,
scanning each car.

Walk past Sainsbury's.
This part of town isn't safe.
Too many people.
Too many chances to be seen,
spied on
and reported.

I weave in and out
of the market stalls,
looking out for aunties.

Traffic lights.

Green.

Cars rolling by.
That's when I spot

her.

Weighed down by a weekly shop,
standing on the opposite side of the street.

I duck down behind Tara,
crouching behind her legs.

I hide.

I mess with my shoelace.
Chin buried into my chest,
eyes down on the tarmac.

I tug on Tara's sock.

Amber?! What are you doing?

That woman knows my dad!

My voice shaky.
My mouth dry.
A bead of sweat
trickles down my back.

So?

I'm not supposed to be out after school, am I!

What can she say?
You were walking around town?!

Yes, that's exactly what she can say!

Tara takes my arm,
pulls me up.

Don't worry.
I don't think she saw you.

Traffic lights change to red
and I sprint across the road,
my legs feeling weak,
shaken by the sighting,
heart thumping like it's
gonna burst out of my chest.

Ten laps of the sports field
haven't got anything on this,
this stomach-churning,
throat-choking
feeling.

I don't scan the cars,
I don't look up,
don't want to catch anyone's eye.
A little bit of sick makes its way up.
I swallow,
burning my throat.

I shoot off.
David catches up,
grabs hold of my hand
and pulls me back.

Even in this panic
I can't help feeling
a tingle in my chest
as his fingers close
round mine.

Time feels like it stops
for a second
before I come back
to reality and pull away.

What the hell do you think you're doing?!

He looks hurt.
His large brown eyes
drawing me in,
making me forget
where I am.

**I just wanted to see if you were OK.
You ran off like a maniac.**

I'd be a lot better if you didn't walk next to me!

I'm so panicked
I don't register
her.

Her
coming out of Wilko's,
another *auntie*
double-taking me,
eyeballing me from across the road
and watching me,
watching me
walking with Tara and
David.

David who won't walk AHEAD like I told him to!

I don't see *her*
till it's too late.

I leg it into a phone shop,
Tara and David
following close behind.

Why are we in here?
You gonna get a phone?
About time!

David's looking all confused
and I'm trying really hard
not to get angry with him.

That woman saw me!
The one with the red jumper . . .
Don't look at her . . . !

I don't think she did, mate.
I think you're being paranoid.
Have you been eating too much bread?

No, Tara!
This isn't anything to do with lactose!

Gluten.

Whatever!

I shakily leave the shop.
I keep my head down.

Traffic lights.

Green.

I can see McDonald's.
Once I'm in there
I know I can relax.

Red . . .

Speed-walk across the road.
Breathe, nearly there.
I'm on a mission,
I'm tunnel vision,
straight towards the safety
of Mackie D's

for now.

MACKIE D'S

I feel too sick to order anything,
my stomach in knots.

The money I stole
from Dad's wallet
when he was passed out
on the couch
still in my pocket.

I roll the note
around in my fingers.

She didn't see me,
I'm imagining it.
She didn't see me,
she didn't see me,
she didn't see me . . .

Tara and David are sitting,
stuffing their faces with nuggets and fries.
I try and have a good time.

Tara's giggling,
she and David sharing private jokes
from their holiday.

I check the time –
my twenty minutes is up.
That's as long as I've got,
can't push it more than that.

I'll pass my lateness off
as a quick chat
with a teacher.

I'll say it's Mrs Wittle.
Dad met her at parents' evening.
She's got purple hair,

Dad will remember her.
He'll believe that.

I've got to go.

David tugs on my sleeve.
Oh, come on, Amber,
stay a bit longer.

Don't give me a hard time, you know I can't.
Plus, didn't you witness the mini heart attack I just had?

He places his hand round my wrist,
I don't resist his hold.
I don't try and pull away.

Five more minutes. Please.

We look at each other.
I'm desperate to tell him how I feel,
try and let my eyes do the talking.

Please.

His hand still on my wrist.

I wish I could.
I know it seems stupid to you.

Nothing you say or do is ever stupid.

His hand slides off my wrist.
Lingers a moment longer on my hand.
It feels *wonderful.*

Do you want me to cleanse your aura before you go?
It'll only take a minute.

No, Tara. I think I'll be OK.

Maybe try and meditate tonight, just so you're not
carrying this energy into a new day.

I take a look at the two of them together.
Sitting side by side.
They look like the perfect couple.

I feel my heart drop
out of my chest,
and I drag it behind me
as I leave.

SPEED TRAINING

Training on the way home
helps take my mind off the lie.

The lie I'm going to have to tell
when I step through the front door.

I take the backstreets and
sprint down a dirty alley,
recover and jog.

Pick up my pace
round the back of the bus garage
and sprint past the park.

Too long.

Stop a quarter of the way.
Catch my breath.
Look behind me,
look in front.

One day.

One day.
I'm gonna sprint
this entire street
without stopping.

Recover and sprint again.

Halfway.
Park seems longer today.

Recover. Sprint again.
Twice more.

Jog up the hill,
turn on to our estate.

I stop.
Take a moment.

Shake out my arms and legs.
Lunge up the front steps.
Long strides,
three steps at a time,
thighs burning
all the way up
to the front door.

Sweaty and smiling,
endorphins helping me forget,
got me seeing through
rose-tinted glasses as I
sneak a peek through the window.

See Dad
sitting at the kitchen table.
It's fine.
I tell myself.

I'm sweaty and smiling,
endorphins still playing their
tricks.

CAUGHT

My key turns
in the front door.
Hands shake
as endorphins start to quit.

I feel them
dying.

Take a deep breath,
try and breathe
life back into them

before I open the door
and walk into the kitchen.

I feel the difference in the air.
It's heavy in here.
All positive feelings disappear,
replaced in an instant
by an almighty lead weight
in my chest.

He stares.
I force a smile
as rocks land in my stomach.

He sits
at the kitchen table.
Eyes bloodshot red.

Where have you been?

School.

Don't lie.

I'm not!

Dad's sitting, staring.

I'll ask you one more time.
Where have you been?

I stayed late talking to my teacher at school.

He rubs his bald head
with clenched fists,
looks at me out of the corner of his eye,
makes his way to the kitchen window and
stares out across the street.

He starts asking too many questions
and I'm telling too many lies.
I say something about Mrs Wittle,
tripping over my words,
as I try to convince.

The one with the purple hair . . .
Small . . .
Parents' evening . . .

Every bit of me is shaking.
A rabbit caught in headlights.
I stand paralysed.

Dad's starting to shout,
saying I was seen with
 . . . a boy.
I swallow vomit

as his voice thunders across the estate,
loud enough for everyone
to hear threats
about *The Man*
across the road.

THE MAN

He lives
across the road.
You can see his house
from the kitchen window.

Ever since we were little
me and Ruby
have been warned
about *The Man* across the road.

How he killed his daughter.
How she'd done bad things.
How she'd shamed the family.

Her parents told the school
she'd gone back to their 'homeland',
but really her dad disposed of the body,
and everyone in the community keeps quiet.

We were to take it as a warning:
should we shame, dishonour or disobey,
we would end up the very same way.

It could be little things like
being caught dancing to the radio.
Or bigger things like
Ruby wanting to do A levels.

I remember the first time
the warning came.
You know The Man across the road . . .
It was almost casual in tone.

I remember thinking,
Why is he telling me?
and then slowly
this sinking feeling . . .
knowing why he was telling me.

So I'd really study The Man.
I'd watch him take his bins out,
wondering if he was disposing of body parts.
I'd spy on him as he mowed his lawn,
wondering if she was buried under the grass.

We always saw him with two daughters,
but if I only saw one daughter,
and I hadn't seen the other one for a while,
I'd get a bit scared, you know . . .

but then she'd reappear,
and I'd be like . . . phew . . .
but then I would think
about the third daughter.

The murdered one,
the one we'd never seen,
and my heart would start beating so fast
I'd find it hard to catch my breath.

A WARNING

When I was little,
he was the monster under my bed,
the bogeyman in the wardrobe,
the demon in the darkness,
the vampire outside my window.

I'd sleep with the light on,
praying I wouldn't become his prey.

Now,
he is real.
The story in the newspaper,
or on the ten o'clock news.
Police ignored girl's pleas.
Remains found in a suitcase.
Father and brother arrested.
An honour killing.

Although
there is no *honour*
in killing.

THREATS

You think because I'm illiterate I don't see?
You think you can pull the wool over my eyes?

Dad's voice
penetrates skin
and bone.

His brow furrowed,
his eyes red,
wild and staring.

His hands
are fists
resting on the table.

You think I don't hear the lie?
You think you can trick me?
You think you're being clever?

My eyes sting
and there's something
in my throat.

Don't cry.
I mustn't cry.

I'm stuck.
Feet buried in the lino,
not listening to the mouth moving,
just the sound ringing in my ears.

Fingers digging into skin.
Pain numbs emotion.

I want to run,
never stopping.

Say something.
You have a tongue.
Speak!

It was just McDonald's.

My voice quiet
weak
frightened.

From now on you come straight home.
Do you know how this makes me look?
Do you know what people will say about me?
Do not put a stain on our family name.

BEHZTI

He talks of dishonour.
Behzti.

You're lucky, he says.
If you were in India,
I would have thrown you
into the street
for behzti like this.

Is it ungrateful to feel
that I'm not that

lucky?

DISHONOUR

Only girls carry behzti.
It is on our shoulders alone.
But behzti stains this family name
by Dad and Dad alone.
Every time he gets drunk
and strangers bring him home.

VOMIT

Legs feel heavy
as they carry me
up the stairs.
My head feels light
as the contents
of my stomach
erupt from my mouth,
filling up the toilet bowl.

INSOMNIA

I sit on the edge
of my bed,
staring at the space
where Ruby's bed
used to be.

The room looks uneven,
feels all wrong,
like it doesn't suit
being half empty.

My eyes close.
I'm so tired.
It feels like
I haven't slept
since she left.

OPPOSITES

Ruby's
gentle
quiet
never makes a fuss.

I'm
spiky
loud
way too emotional.

We were more than sisters.
We were allies.

We saw the hurdles we were
to overcome,
and we were going to jump them together.

I'd tell Ruby
that she could do with getting
a bit of fire in her belly.

She'd say
I could do with simmering down.

Couldn't be more different,
some would say.

I thought we complemented each other.

We didn't have to try.
We just belonged.
We fitted.

That's what made us work.

That's what made us

STRONG.

THINGS I MISS ABOUT RUBY

Sharing a room.
(Sharing a room
with Ruby was the best.)

Telling her everything.
(She was the first friend
I ever made.)

Nights tucked up in her bed.
(Because I was too scared to
sleep alone.)

Ruby tucked up in my bed.
(Reading to me
until I slept.)

Making vision boards together.
(We loved to dream. Places
to travel, goals to achieve.)

Supporting each other.
(She'd time my sprints,
I'd read every essay she wrote.)

Dancing on her feet.
(She would carry me around
and call me her little dolly.)

Feeling safe.
(When Mum and Dad would argue,
she'd take me upstairs, pile duvets over me
and put earmuffs over my ears.)

The things we said before we went to sleep.
(Love you like apple loves crumble.
Love you like sock loves foot.)

LOVE—HATE

Ruby was my strength.
I felt superhuman
knowing she was around.

Ruby was my everything,
more than a sister, a forever friend.
It was us against the world.

Together we spied on *The Man*.
Squealed if he came out of his house
and ducked down from the kitchen window.

Laughing to mask the fear,
knowing I was safe with her.
She'd squeeze my hand tight as we passed

by his house on the way to school
only letting go when
she knew I felt safe.

We shared dreams of the future and
played games of make-believe,
telling ourselves,
It won't always be like this.

Promising to protect each other.
Standing side by side.
No one would ever break us.

Now we fight
like *they* fight.

We torture and hurt.
With a swift slice of a sharp tongue,

we open old wounds and
stop them from healing.

Years of lessons
impossible to unlearn.

We fight like they fight.
We **fight** like they fight.
We fight like **they** fight.
We fight like they **fight**.

And we are *good.*

RUBY'S BROKEN PROMISES

I'll always be here for you,
she said.
I'll never leave you
to fend for yourself,
she said.
Trust me,
she said.
I'll get us out of here,
she said.

Then she left.

WHAT'S EASIER?

Is it easier
to lose someone
for real?
To bury them
in the ground,
never see them again?

Rather than
seeing them
but never
having them back
the way they were?

To have them
living,
breathing,
but gone?

OVERWHELMED

My head is a jumble of images
a mixing desk of sounds.

The Man Auntie Vomit Traffic Lights Fists Sprinting Tara
bewakoofbewakoofbewakoofbewakoofbewakoofbewakoofbewakoof
Red Jumper Green Light Track Shoelace Tarmac Sweat Trainers
vomitvomitvomitvomitvomitvomitvomitvomitvomitvomitvomitvomit.
Woman. Staring. Eyes. David. Hand. Wrist. Eyes.
Shopping Bags Phone Shop Mackie D's Heart Thumping
Thudthudthudthudthudthudthudthudthudthud
Hand Wrist Warm Stay Smile Eyes Cheekbones Hand Wrist Warm Stay
DavidDavidDavidDavidDavidDavidDavidDavidDavidDavidDavidDavid
T   H   E   M   A   N
deaddaughterdeaddaughterdeaddaughterdeaddaughterdeaddaughter
Can'tbreathecan'tbreathecan'tbreathecan'tbreathecan'tbreathe

H   E   L   P

Can'tbreathecan'tbreathecan'tbreathecan'tbreathecan'tbreathe
can'tbreathe can'tbreathecan'tbreathecan'tbreathecan'tbreathe
can'tbreathecan'tbreathe

H   E   L   P

Inhale exhale inhale exhale inhale exhale inhale exhale inhale exhale
I   DON'T   WANT   TO   BE   HERE
Inhale exhale inhale exhale inhale exhale inhale exhale inhale exhale
Revolutions traffic lights purple hair park toilet vomit fake pupils eyes
track running
RunningRunningRunningRunningRunningRunningRunningRunning
I   WISH   I   COULD   ESCAPE
BehztiBehztiBehztiBehzti
clawingclawingclawingclawingclawingclawingclawingclawingclawing

GET   ME   OUT
bewakoofbewakoofbewakoofbewakoofbewakoofbewakoofbewakoof

H   E   L   P

Help
Help
Help
Anyone?

RESTRICTIONS

If I can't run,
I'm not whole.
I'm only half
a person.

The thought of that
weighs heavy,
seems so dark.

The feeling goes
beyond running.

I see
my entire future
like Ruby's.

The realization
that choice
is not a privilege
I am given.

The frustration of
wanting more
and not knowing
how to get it.

I'm paralysed
with fear,
allowing only tears
the freedom
to

run
down
my
face.

LONGING FOR BEFORE

I stare at the ceiling,
longing for a time
before
I wanted more.

Before
I stopped being content.
Before
I learned that girls had to be subservient.
Before
I decided that being subservient

just isn't in my blood.

HOMEWORK

The flimsy, dog-eared book
feels heavy in my hand.

I stare at the cover,
the title teasing.

The Art of Revolution.
I turn to the introduction.

Fighting for freedom.
To do what the heart desires.

I begin reading,
sinking deeper and deeper,

devouring each page.
Something is calling.

I feel it running through me,
testing, teasing, telling me

that what's to come will be
the biggest, bravest thing

I will ever do.

STAGES

One to eight.
It's all there:
the secrets
the plots
the war
the change
the peace.

Words land in my empty stomach,
nourishing it with tales of courage
that starve the ever-present
baseline of fear and anxiety as I
immerse myself in stage one and

how it all starts.

REREADING

People

                                            restless

              held down

                                                restrictions

                  forced to accept less

bitterness

                                            GROWING

Words leap out
from the page
and land like a
punch in the gut,
waking up my insides.

I flick through
the pages,
trying to absorb
the text as quick as I can,
drink it all in.

The only other place
I am this excited
is on the track.
I'm amazed –
Mr History Jones
has won me over.
I take it all back . . .

I feel truly alive.

A KNOWING

Knowing   that change must come from me.
Knowing   I do have a choice.
Knowing   that this choice,
                        that this change,
                        might mean
                        my life
                        may never
                        be the
                        same again.

MEDITATE

I light Tara's gift.
The smell of sage
wraps itself round the room.
I close my eyes.

Breathe in
two–three–four
breathe out
two–three–four.

Tara taught me
how to meditate.

I'm no good.

Breathe in
two–three–four
breathe out
two–three–four.

Breathe in
two–three–four
breathe out
two . . .

It's no good.
Thoughts keep racing.

I'm too restless.
Too angry.
Too impatient.
Too full of rage.
Too ready to

REBEL.

TWO
DISSATISFACTION

ANATOMY OF
A REVOLUTION
STAGE 2

Dissatisfaction spreads.

Frustration burrows
into the hearts and minds
of yet-to-be-born leaders.

A new movement begins.

OVERWORKED

Mum is home at
6.45 p.m. on the dot.
Meditation turned to sleep,
the slam of the door
jars me awake.

I make my way downstairs
from the bedroom
I've been hiding in
since Dad's threats.

Bags of shopping
by the front door.

The smell of sweat
wafts past me as
she places her tiffin box
and empty flask
by the sink.

Mum's face
drenched with
exhaustion.

Her body bent
by the weight
of being overworked
and underpaid.

RITUAL

Mum doesn't always
know what she's buying.
She can memorize packaging
but packaging can change.
So I translate the receipt,
read it out loud.

It's a ritual of sorts.

**Two lots of four-pint milk,
two pounds and ten pence.
One bag of sugar, seventy-five pence.
Two Colgate, three pounds . . .
it wasn't buy one get one free,
it was buy two for three pounds.
They're normally one ninety-nine each . . .
you got a pound off,
it's still good.
Ribena, eighty-nine pence,
twelve-pack of crisps, one pound twenty,
yep, half price . . .
PG Tips, ninety-nine pence.
Cornflakes, forty-nine pence,
(urgh, Tesco Value) . . . nothing . . .
yes, they are a good brand,
it's fine, cheaper is better.
Twelve eggs, seventy-nine pence,
two loaves of bread reduced, thirty pence each . . .
So that came to ten pounds and eighty-one pence.
You gave eleven pounds and
you got nineteen pence change.**

And now
she can
relax.

ILLITERACY

Mum and Dad
can't read or write
in English or Punjabi.
They can say the odd
word in English,
but that's about it.

They could.
There are classes.
He is too proud and
he won't allow her to learn.

This way
she can't read the posters
telling her she
doesn't have to put up
with the abuse.

This way
she can't read
the leaflets
telling her
where's safe.

CHAI 1

A cup for each person.
Me, Mum, Dad.
Three cups of water
into a saucepan.
Waiting . . . patiently
for the spices to mingle
and provide a provocation
of smells.
A pinch of cinnamon
to stoke the tension,
a teaspoon of fennel seeds
to raise a voice,
a teaspoon of carom seeds
to break a dish,
three green cardamom
to upturn a chair,
one large black cardamom
to stand your ground,
a pinch of arrowroot
to throw a punch,
three slices of fresh ginger
to heal a wound.

CHAI 2

Dad: **Not too much arrowroot – it was bitter last time.**

I obey.
Make sure I put in
half the amount.

How much did you make today?

The spiced water starts to simmer.
Add three teabags.

Mum: I'm not sure. Amber will work it out.

Well, was it a busy day?

It's always busy.

The tea begins to boil.

I think I made the same as yesterday.

Turn the heat down.
Leave to simmer.

Add milk,
as much as you desire.
Leave to boil.

Dad tells Mum about
my after-school 'escapade'.

The milky tea starts to heat up.

Mum listens.
Gives me a sideways glance.

The milky tea starts to boil.

She's saying something about it being *OK*.

Something about me *not doing it again.*
My frustration grows.

I forget to watch the tea.
It boils over.
Sizzling on the flames,
a light brown froth covers the hotplate.

The tea!

Stupid girl!

It's OK.

Stupid girl. You were standing right next to it.

Don't worry.

Then simmer.

After thirty minutes,
you have chai.

The house is soaked
with the scent of spices.
There's a comfort in the smell.

Pour into mugs
through a sieve
to collect the spices.

Wait for Dad to take
the first sip . . .

It'll do.

Discard the spice
and breathe.

This hour is usually quiet.

PROBLEM CHILD

Out of me and Ruby,
Mum says
I'm the one
she worries about
the most.

You know what he's like. Just be good.
Be good.

BE. GOOD.

The nature of my tiny disobedience
compared to the scale of the consequences
makes my blood boil.

MUM'S MANTRA	MY MANTRA
Do as you're told.	*I have my own mind and will use it.*
Keep your head down.	*I will be loud and proud.*
Cover up.	*Scream and strip naked!*
Don't talk too loudly.	*I have a voice, it will be heard.*
Be small.	*I will not apologize for my existence.*
Don't answer back.	*I am not a robot.*
Don't question.	*I will not be silenced.*
What you say and do reflects on our position in the community.	*I will not let your fear dictate my future*
It's not your life, it's your parents' life.	*I have one life, I intend to live it.*

BIG TALK

In reality
Mum's mantra
is also my mantra.

A DAY'S WORK

Write my work in my book, Mum says.

I take her tatty workbook out
from the kitchen drawer.
Her eyes closed,
her body swaying into sleep.

Twelve hours, no, eleven, they don't count lunch,
three pounds twenty an hour.

After a quick
tap tap tap
on the calculator,

Thirty-five pounds and twenty pence.

It will pay for the week's shopping. She yawns.

Didn't you get paid today?

Tomorrow. Some problem at the bank.

What kind of problem?

I don't know.
Like they tell us anything.
The manager said tomorrow.

Dad looks irritated.
Mum's eyes start to close
as she drifts into sleep.

PAIN

I watch Mum sleep on the settee in the kitchen.
Eyes always closing before she has a chance to finish her tea.

Everything always hurts, she says. Her hips, legs, arms, back.
Everything always hurts so I try and make it better.

I rub her feet and massage her legs. It's fine, she'll say.
Physical pain always heals, it's the emotional pain that stays.

MADE IN BRITAIN

These factories
are **S**ecret.
True colours
hidden
in toxic dy**e**
used to colour
expensive garments.

Zero-hour,
underpaid,
no **C**ontracts,
no rights.

Fear and
intimidation
keeping worke**r**s
in check.

They pr**e**y
on desperate
people. Unaware,
unknowing **t**hat
even in their ignorance
more is possible.

An under**W**orld
of fast fashion
filling up sh**O**pping centres
and high streets.

Ha**r**d work.
Illegal work.
Dangerous wor**k**.

A MIX OF THE TWO

Dad at the kitchen table,
controlling the space,
sitting on his throne.

Me and Mum on the settee,
springs digging into
bum cheeks.

We sit,
not talking,
just the sound
of slurping tea
from mugs
echoing over the tense
atmosphere.

Mum's feet in my lap,
the skin on her heels
hard and yellow.
Deep cracks around the outside,
like her feet want to split,
break into little pieces
and escape
any which way they can.

Mum's so small.
So thin.
Lately I think she looks thinner.

Ruby definitely takes after Mum.
Relatives would say she's the
spitting image.
Delicate features
with Mum's quiet soul.

I'm a mix of Mum and Dad.

Aunties would take it in turns
to say which bit
I get from each parent.

I have Mum's almond eyes,
Dad's straight nose,
her thin lips,
his dimpled chin

and I'm not there yet
but
I'm going to have Dad's height.

It makes sense.

I've always felt
like there were
two people fighting
to get out of me.

X

X marks the spot
where Mum and Dad
should sign their names,
if they knew how,
on the letter
giving consent
for the school geography trip.

There's a school trip next term.
I just need one of you to sign this.

Dad is immediately suspicious.
Where, what, who with?

Peak District.
To look at rocks.
School.

Dad thinks about it
and puts an 'X' by the X
telling you where to sign.
I will sign it on their behalf later,
this is just a formality.

I should teach you to write your name.

Dad scoffs.
I don't need you to teach me anything.
Am I the adult or are you?

Well, what about Mum?

Her eyes light up.

She doesn't need to learn anything either.

Mum is silent.
Looks down at her now-cold tea.

He picks up his coat and
leaves for the pub.

She waits a minute or two.

Is he down the road?

I look out of the kitchen window.

Yep, nearly at the bottom of the street.

Good.

She takes a little brown envelope
out of her bag.
She opens it
and begins to count the money inside.
She takes
forty pounds out of the bundle,
Can't have him drink it all away,
and stuffs it into her bra.

Boosted by her rebellion,
she says,
Write my name in English.
I just want to see what it looks like.

I take a piece of paper
and write her name
in large capitals in thick black pen.

What are the letters?

I read them out.

S U R I N D E R   R A I

She stares at the piece of paper.

He's right. It's too late for me to learn new things now.

No it's not.

I get another piece of paper.

Watch, I say,
and start copying out the letters.

Mum watches.
I give her a pen and paper.

Your turn.

She places the tip of the pen on the paper.
She hesitates.
An unease creeps across her face.

I'm tired.

Just try.

Some other time.

Try.

Leave it, I said!

Fear turns to anger
and that's the end of that.

ANGER

A substitute emotion.

As in,
people make themselves

angry

so they don't
feel

pain.

TRAINERS

I think about
asking her for
new trainers.

I know what
the answer will be.
The money she

has is to
pay the bills
and buy food.

If she left it
to Dad,
we'd be eating

tins of baked beans
in candlelight
and having

cold baths.
So I search
the drawers for

superglue.

SUNSET

I watch the sun setting,
a moment
that brings beauty

to the concrete jungle outside.

Grey walls
craving to be coloured
soak up red and pink hues.

Tonight it's particularly beautiful.

A deep ruby red.
Lifeless structures haloed
in a crimson light.

A reminder that beauty
can be found in the
starkest of places.

Red sky at night,
Ruby's delight, we'd say.
Ruby would say it was a sign

my wishes would
come true in the morning.

Training with the athletics team.
It might not be a problem,
I think.

I allow myself to dream.

I see Ruby's car pull up outside.
If it wasn't for baby Tiya,
I'd HATE her visits.

Yes, hate is a strong word
but it applies to Ruby these days.

EGGSHELLS

Bad moods
follow Ruby around
like a bad smell.

Her husband, Jas, is a quiet man.
She gives me Tiya before
she's through the door.

Like Tiya's a dirty dishcloth
she can't wait to get rid of.
Jas gives me a sympathetic smile.

Tiya puts her chunky arms
round my neck.
Bamber, she says
and snuggles into my shoulder.

Mum quickly sits up.
Starts tidying her hair,
apologizes for sleeping.

I am ordered to
make tea and serve snacks.
I empty a packet of biscuits on to a plate.
I pour Bombay mix into bowls.

Jas insists I don't have to
run around after him.

It's fine,
I say, putting down the plate of biscuits
a little louder than I should.

How is school? Jas asks.

**All right. My teacher wants me on the athletics team.
She says I'm the fastest in the year.**

That's brilliant! he says.

Ruby's face hardens.
Like running's going to get you anywhere,
she spits.

I didn't say it was!
I'm just repeating what my teacher said! I snap.

We stare.
Fired up
for a fight.

Jas tries his best
to extinguish
the flames
by blowing raspberries
on Tiya's stomach.

My heart
used to ache.
I tried to help.

But she became hard.
Stopped talking,
so I stopped trying.

Now I've become
as hard as her.

MARRIAGE

It wasn't her choice.

She said I was too
young to understand,
but I did.

It wasn't her choice.

She talked of honour
and respecting our parents.
I screamed in her face.
Told her that it's her life
and she should marry
who she wants
when she wants.

I begged her to fight.
She didn't.

That was her choice.

I feel as though I've always known
from the moment I was born
that this life without choice,
this life of duty,
was not for me.

The day she said *yes*
to the wedding
a split occurred,
so violent
that nothing I said
or did offered any

comfort.

I wanted to drop down into
the crevasse that
had been created
and disappear forever.
Overnight we became

strangers.

We are broken
in ruins,
a once unbreakable bond
in disrepair,
unable to find the pieces
to put ourselves back together

again.

JAS

He is proof
that not all men
are the same.

RUBY'S TRICK 1

Jas is in awe of Ruby.
He says she's the brains.
Says she deserves more
than the shoe shop.

She rolls her eyes,
tells him to shut up.

Then her eyes will fill up
and the corners of
the whites turn red.

She'll put her hands
to her face,

pressing her fingers
to her eyes.

Classic Ruby trick.

Pretending to yawn.
Pretending to rub her eyes

when really she's soaking up tears
through her fingertips.

TIYA

No one **G**ave gifts when Tiya was born.

No one d**I**d anything. There were

no celeb**R**ations,

no temp**L**e blessing. Instead they mourned

like it wa**S** a funeral.

EAVESDROPPING

I watch Tiya
run round the living room
as I flick through TV channels.

I hope you don't have to put up with the same stuff I do.
I hope it's different for you.

She looks at me
with her chubby round
innocent face.

I hope you can be whatever you want to be.

She turns away
and continues to play,
too young to understand
the walls that are built round her.

Every now and then
I hear the word 'wedding'.
I hear the words
'need to watch her'.

There is a tightness in my chest.
A quickness in my breath.
An anger in my blood.

RISE

Maybe –
it's always been there
waiting –
for the right time.

A fight.
I deserve more,
something whispers
deep inside.

I look at Tiya.

For you.
I'll fight so you won't have to.

REBEL

To **R**ise.

To **E**xercise your rights.

To **B**reak through resistance.

To **E**xpostulate.

To **L**ead the revolt.

DAD'S BACK 1

Turn the volume down,
turn the telly off.
Don't say a word.
Can't he wait?
Five minutes,
just five minutes.
He stands in the doorway, swaying.

Mum – exhausted –
rolls out chapattis.

Ruby stirs the curry,
I serve,

Dad eats,
Jas eats.

I want to
scream   *the*   *house*   *down.*

A WORRY

I worry I'm like him.
I'm becoming him.

I look at my father
and wonder what
happened
to turn him
into the man
he is and how it

trickled
down
to
me.

Is that how it starts?
A silent anger
bubbling inside,
simmering,
waiting like a
dormant volcano
until one day
it erupts
and you're
no longer
in control.

CHICKEN

When Ruby and Jas leave,
I try to pick my moment.

I have the form in my hand.
I study his mood.

On a scale of one to ten how drunk is he?
Eight.
On a scale of one to ten how brave am I feeling?
Zero.

I have a few weeks till half-term.

I have time.

LETTERS

Dad waves letters
in front of my face.
Read these, he slurs.

Three are junk mail.
One is in a brown envelope.

Something about brown envelopes
makes me nervous.

Brown envelopes are always
important. Official.

If it's important,
if it's official,
and I get the important
and official information wrong,

I'll be
in big trouble.

MEMORY

I am eight.

I sit nervously,
taking on the fear of a father
who is embarrassed he can't do this himself.
But my Punjabi's not as good as my English.
One language taking over the other,
I sit soaking up anxiety like a sponge,
carrying it around,
heavy and drenched,
unsettling my insides.
Facts wash around in my head.
Wringing out the information
as best as I can remember
only for some bits
to be dribbled out incorrectly.

When you have illiterate parents,
everything falls on you.
No matter how young,
you become the parent too.

THE BROWN ENVELOPE

The important letter
is from the council.
They are cutting
our benefits.

I fear Dad will
fly into a rage.

But instead
we all sit in silence.

The air feels thick
and heavy with desperation.

A sense of impending doom.

There must be a mistake.
Call tomorrow.
Make an appointment,
he demands
while picking up his coat,
muttering
bewakoof, nikame
under his breath
as he leaves,
slamming the door,
making the whole house
shake with his rage.

LONGING

I lie on my bed,
staring at my wardrobe,
notice how it's
leaning to one side.

Doesn't have the
other one to lean against,
doesn't have Ruby's
bed to prop it up.

Ruby would always
fix everything.
A bit of cardboard under there,
a bit of superglue here.

The loneliness is drowning.

I feel like there's a hole in my chest
and all the darkness is seeping in.

I wish for a time
I could bury myself
in my mother's arms
and she'd rock away the tears.

Or cuddle up in bed with
Ruby and her stories.

Or have Dad hold me
high above his head,
flying me round the room,
making aeroplane noises.

I wish for that time.

SCARED

Write your truth.
I try to start on
my English assignment.

Write your truth.
I see Mr Walker
already disappointed,
already writing a big fat
F on my work.

Write your truth.
The words send spikes
rushing into every corner,
irritating skin and bone.

I stare at the blank page,
unable to start.
The muscles in my hand
seem locked.
I shake. Not cold.
Scared if I reveal too much
I'll open myself up,
turn inside out,
and Mr Walker
will see everything.

See me.
See it all.

My truth

is not
mine

to tell.

ARGUMENT

I hear the front door slam.
I hear Dad shouting my name.

Amber! Amber!
You call tomorrow. You hear me.
You call the Jobcentre tomorrow.
You sort this out, do something useful for once.
Why else do we bother sending you to school!

I don't answer.
He's not looking for an answer.
It pays to be silent.

Leave her alone. She said she would.
She needs to study.

Why does Mum answer back?
She knows what he's like.
She provokes him.

Fear buries the guilt
that surrounds
these words.

Was I talking to you?
How dare you answer back,
I wasn't talking to you!

I press my hands against my ears
and begin reading out loud . . .

'A rebellion is an act of open resistance
against an established authority . . .'

I read louder and louder
as voices are raised . . .

'A revolt seeks to overthrow and destroy . . .'

as objects are shattered . . .

'A rebellion is an act of resistance. A revolt seeks revolution . . .'

until there is quiet.

I open my bedroom door.
I creep downstairs,

see her on the settee,
head shrouded in a shawl.
Hands in prayer,
rocking

back and forth
back and forth.

I check her face.
Wipe her tears,
search for bruises.

I put my arm round her.
She feels hard.
My embrace
makes her wince.

I hold her tight,
try to melt
her tough exterior
with the warmth of my embrace
no matter how much
she might resist.

REBELS

The history books
demand my attention.

They seem to ground me
in the chaos somehow.

I begin reading about heroes
that rocked the status quo.

Those who had visions of liberation
that were bigger than themselves.

Those who vowed to fight
for change above all else.

From a picture, a man with wavy hair
and flat cap stares back at me.

It's not just about me wanting to run away.
The fight is bigger than that.

If I go, Mum has to come with me.

DAYDREAMING

Mum and I
stand up to Dad.
We overthrow his regime.

It won't be easy.
He will resist.
But we fight back.

We are cleverer than him.
We leave this house
for a better one.

A house on a tree-lined street
and wide-open
spaces around us.

She reads.
She writes.
She has friends.

I run
      I run
            I run

and we are safe.

NIGHT-DREAMING

Tossing and turning
mind racing
athletics club
Dad
fights
threats
Mum
crying
Mum
Mum
Mum
revolt
destroy
Ruby
Tiya
Dad
revolt
destroy
The Man
threats
David
Tara
David
Tara and David
their holiday
them
together
whispering
athletics
them
together
athletics
them together
heart-breaking
heart-breaking
heart-breaking.

MORNING

Seven a.m.
alarm.
Snooze for another ten.

Slept too badly
for it to be morning.

Slink under the covers.
Wrap the duvet round my head.
Tight.
Battling instincts,
fighting thoughts.

Today is a good day.

Whatever.
Slink down further,
try and catch the words
before they
fall
through
the
cracks
in my heart.
Try and catch them
before they are
engulfed by coffin dreams.
I sink.
Not breathing.

ALARM!

Can't be ten minutes already?
Went too quick.
I stare at the clock.
It stares right back.
Seven ten a.m.
I throw it.
Pissed off.

It hits my shelves,
knocks Ruby's old A-level guides.
Next time she comes over
I'm gonna throw them at her.
Tell her to take them home.

I emerge.
Check the clock.
Seven twelve a.m.
I want to get back into bed,
can't face this day.

No sports today.
Just a normal day

swimming in my own thoughts.

HOME GYM

Fourteen stairs
between the ground
and first floor
of our home.

My mini playground.
My gym.
My weekly circuit session.

Not allowed out
so got to learn to be

inventive.

Jump lunges,
sprints up and down the stairs,
lunge up the stairs two at a time,
hop up,
jump down,
jump squats.

The possibilities are endless.
Sprint up two at a time and
back down again.
Repeat ten, twenty, thirty times.

When I'm puffed out,
I stand at the kitchen window,
glugging down a glass of water.
Look out at the undulating streets,
knowing the arboretum
lies just beyond.

Wishing I could get my trainers on
and run down there.
Smell the fresh air,
feel the wind on my face.

I see *The Man* across the road.
He stands in his front garden,
looking at his red roses.

My heart thumps with fear.
I take a final gulp of water
and do ten more sprints.

BREAKFAST

One Weetabix,
one teaspoon of sugar,
milk,
half a banana,
one cup of sweet chai.

Pour me some tea.
Make me toast.
Put cheese on it.
Hurry up.

Dad's demanding.
Been up an hour himself.
Can't put bread in the toaster.
Can't make tea.

He'll wait.
As long as it takes
till I come down the stairs.

I'm the one needing to get somewhere.
Where's he got to be?
Oh yeah,
the bench outside Tesco
where he'll sit till dinnertime,
watching,
keeping guard over the town's daughters and wives.

I do as I'm told.
Although these days I'm not so polite.
I'm getting angry.
Can't help it.
I stomp.
Huff.
Close cupboard doors a bit louder.
Slam plates down harder.

Making breakfast for someone
is not that big a deal
in itself . . .
It takes less than twenty seconds to put bread in the toaster.
Less than thirty seconds to butter it.
Less than sixty seconds to cut some cheese
and place it on the toast.
That's less than a minute and a half of my day . . .

It's the principle.

'A situation that requires something be done a certain way
because one believes it is the only right way.'

Dad believes I should make his breakfast
because I'm a girl.
That's what girls are born to do.
To serve.
His words.
Not mine.

I wouldn't mind making his breakfast
if he made mine sometimes,
if he didn't *expect* me to make his.

I don't mind doing things for other people.
But I do mind when I'm doing it because
I am less than.

It's the principle of the matter,
and therefore

it **IS** a big deal.

MORNING ADMIN

Since Ruby left
this is down to me.

Speaking to official people
makes me nervous.

The sound of
classical music
while on hold
unsettles my breakfast.

Dad sits with me,
watching and waiting.

The earliest appointment,
he reminds me
for the tenth time.

I try and make one
for the weekend
but the offices are closed.

Next week is the earliest.
Tuesday morning.
Nine a.m.

Appointment made
and I'm annoyed
that I'll be missing school.

I can't miss school. This year is important.

He ignores me.
Pours himself a whisky
and shuffles upstairs.

GREEN-EYED MONSTER 2

Finally out of the door.
Cut through the estate,
dodge the dog shit,
past the garage,
the chippy,
the corner shop,
up the hill,
try and beat my time.
Carrying books telling tales
of revolutionary rebels
puts a fighting spring
in my step.

I see Tara and David talking
outside the school gates,
looking all cosy,
and just like that
courage twists into jealousy.

NO MORE RISKS

Mackie D's later, yeah?

David holds my arms out
like a master puppeteer,
dancing round me,
playing the nerd.

No way.
That lady saw me yesterday
and called the house.

You're joking!

He drops my arms
and looks at me
in disbelief.

It's OK.
I'm OK.

I'm so sorry.

She did tell you to walk ahead, David.
Tara strokes my arm.
I'm sorry, Amber . . .

It's OK, it's not your fault.
I knew it was a risk.

Was everything OK?
I know your dad can be really strict.

Just the usual.

I'm embarrassed.
These two worlds colliding
and I'm in the middle, suffocating.

I'm sorry, Amber.
I should know better.
My mum tells me all these stories
about when she was dating my dad
and all the sneaking around they had to do.
Scary shit.

If only your parents were like Ravneet's parents.
They know she's dating Paul and they've invited him
round to dinner.

Tara looks at me like she's had the best idea.
Her eyes sparkling with excitement.

Maybe your parents could meet Ravneet's parents
and they could knock some sense into
your mum and dad?! Tell them to chill out.

Yeah, right.
You should hear what
the aunties down the temple say about
Rav and her parents!

Same thing they say about my mum?

Er . . . I dunno,
I say.
Unable to hide the truth.
Wearing the lie on my face
like the make-up
plastered on the *cool girls'* faces
because I know what everyone says
about David's mum, Beena.

It's OK, my mum knows.

Beena ran away from home
when she was sixteen.
She runs a women's refuge
and a community centre,
helping women like her,
who have to run away
from abusive families or partners.

She has the biggest heart
of anyone you will ever meet.
But at the temple she is
talked about like she is dirt.

She may have run
miles from her home
but communities are small
and communities talk.

The school bell rings.
We walk up the steps
towards our form room.

I wish we could all hang out after school.

Yeah, me too.

Me three.
I'll eat a cheeseburger for you!

Don't use me as an excuse to stuff your face!
One day, guys, I'm gonna fly.
I'm gonna fly so friggin' far away.
I'll walk down the street
and go where I like,
and no one will care.

David looks at me
like he really believes it.
I'm sure he's going
to put his arm round me.

Correction.

I want him to put
his arm round me.

He hesitates.
Taps me on the shoulder
and puts his hands
in his pockets.

Yeah. You will.

REGISTRATION

Tara heads to the science block
and I'm humanities.

See you at break!

Tara runs off.
Meets up with Sharon, Daljit, Martin and Steph.
They don't like me much.
Tara told me they said I was hard-faced.
She told me to smile more.
Which I hate.
Makes me want to smile less.

Just me and David left
and I'm lost for words.

Cheer up. It's gonna be OK.
My mum says if you want something bad enough
you can get it. Just got to work out a way.
Fancy coming to mine for lunch?

Yeah, that would be great.

I catch him staring at Tara.

Hey, if I can find a way to join the athletics team again,
we'll be training to–

Sorry, I forgot to ask Tara something . . .

–gether.

He runs off,
catching up with Tara.
I'm on my own.
Try not to stare at
Tara and David deep in conversation.
That's when I see *her*.
Gemma.

She tries not to make eye contact.
A voice in my head tells me to:
Leave her alone.
You don't want to have that effect on someone,
I see it at home too often.

I can't help it.
I'm angry she won't stare back,
look me in the eye,
angry she's being a victim,

and then something else takes over.

Travels into my veins,
into my bones,
changing me from the inside,
like I'm not *me* any more,
can't hear the *nice* voice,
the voice saying,

That's what Mum does,
Mum looks down,
Mum looks down,
Mum looks down.

Instead I'm smiling,
pushing past her
as we enter the classroom.

Bitch.
You wanna watch it.

CAUSE AND EFFECT

Mr History Jones
splits the class in two.
He jumps between

the two sides,
pointing and yelling,
getting us to

shout out the long-
and short-term causes
of the European revolutions of 1848.

Unrest can be
simmering for
years.

Then one day
one moment
blows the lid.

One event
triggers
the downfall.

Something inside me
is waking up,
teasing me.

Are you ready?
it whispers.
It's coming.

Be ready.

DABBAWALLAS

I sit impatiently
through English,
maths
and French.

In geography
we watch a video
about dabbawallas in India.

Most of them are illiterate
but they've got this amazing system
of colour-coding and signs.

Taking tiffins early in the morning
from wives in their homes
to bicycles,
trains,
and to their husbands'
workplaces for lunch,
and then all the way back again
by the evening.

Everyone in class agrees
how brilliant it is,
and I say,

That's what my mum does.

Mr Geography Jones looks confused,
takes a moment to collect his thoughts.

Your mother makes your father's tiffin box?

**No, she colour-codes everything in the pantry,
cos she can't read the tins.**

Oh. Does she have a problem with her eyesight?

No, she can't –

I'm regretting opening
my mouth . . .

– read.

A deadly silence,
followed by an eruption of laughter.
Even Gemma's got a smirk on her face.
Mr Geography Jones just stands there staring,
looking slightly horrified.

I don't get it.
A minute ago,
everyone was saying
how brilliant
the dabbawallas were.

DAVID'S FOR LUNCH

David lives in a house
on a tree-lined street.

His house has high ceilings
which makes it feel like

there's more oxygen.
Breathing feels easier,

and my brain feels lighter,
as we relax on a sofa

that's bigger than my bed.
Beena is home, which always makes me happy.

You have to try and rise above it.

That doesn't help, Tara!
You wouldn't be saying that if it was you!

Tara's just trying to help . . .

A sudden stab of jealousy
pierces my stomach.

Hey, hey, what's going on?

Beena walks into the lounge
with a tray full of sandwiches and juice.

Why all the shouting?

I tell her about class,
about the dabbawallas,
the embarrassment.

I wouldn't have said anything,
but everyone kept going on about how brilliant they were
and – I don't know – I felt proud . . .

You should be.
I know a lot of women in your mum's position.

It's so weird people can't read and write in this day and age.

David screws up his face like
he's trying to make sense of it all.
I notice Tara nudge him in the ribs.

Ow! What?

Tara rolls her eyes.
I feel instantly guilty
for snapping at her earlier.

They're a product of their environment is all.
It's a complex situation,

Beena looks at me
with the warmth
I used to get from Ruby.

Try and get your mum to come to the community centre.
We've just started running another English class.
It would be great for her to meet new people.

I'll ask her.

David tells me you're on the athletics team again.

Yeah, I'm not sure I can this year.
Dad doesn't approve.

You can if you want to.

Easier said than done.

This is your life, Amber. It's your one chance. I'm not saying it's easy, believe me, I know, but nothing worth doing ever is.

You don't know my dad.

I think I do. Sounds exactly like my situation when I was growing up. Don't let anyone get in the way of your dreams. Sooner or later you have to make a choice. What life do you want to live? What kind of woman do you want to become?

BEENA

She's that girl.
Fell in love at fifteen girl.
Pregnant at sixteen girl.
She's that girl.
The one who everyone talks about girl.
The one who can't shake off her past girl.
The one everyone fears girl.
Because she's not ashamed girl.
The proud girl.
Despite her past girl.
The one they wish would disappear girl.
The fighter girl.
The one who can corrupt girl.
Holds her head up girl.
Sticks her middle finger up girl.
Laughs too loudly girl.
Doesn't know her place girl.
Should know her place girl.
Takes up space girl.
Proudly stands tall girl.
Not moving for no one girl.
Not apologizing for nothing girl.
Owning her right to be here girl.
Not cowering girl.
Lifting up others girl.
Giving the voiceless a voice girl.
Despite everything she survived girl.

And boy does that scare some folk.

A PRODUCT OF THE ENVIRONMENT...

means that the person you are
is a direct result of how you grew up.

The environment that you were brought up in
influences the decisions you make now.

Your environment makes you who you are.
Tara and David have grown up with books and computers,

with parents who take an interest in their studies.
This means they are more likely to become successful.

Mum and Dad were brought up in a poor village.
Now they are illiterate. Unable to get good jobs,

which is why we live where we live, why Dad drinks
and why Mum believes she isn't worth more.

Ruby and I have grown up in a home where violence is the norm.
This means we may be at greater risk of depression

and of being violent ourselves. Because of where we live we are
less likely to have successful careers or go on to higher education.

This is all part of a bigger problem with *the system*. There are stories
of *exceptionalism*. People who break away from the system.

Can I break away?

If so,
how?

SECRET TALKS

We drag
our feet
back to school.

I notice Gemma
hanging out by the canteen and
the embarrassment comes flooding back.

Stupid cow.
I'll teach her to laugh at me again.

Just leave her.

Tara's right – let it go.

But she deserves it
after what she did.

I notice a look they give each other.
A look that indicates
they've spoken about this
and I wonder how many other secret conversations
they've been having behind my back.

BACK HOME

I   slowly   make   my   way   home.

Raised voices.

I hear them before
I reach the front door.

My dad's voice booms
through the estate.

It vibrates
the walls.

Windowpanes tremble
with thunderous tones.

Mum makes a sound that pierces
like a bolt of lightning.

I dread opening the door,
knowing the storm that rages inside.

The lady next door threatens to call the police.
I ignore her, hoping she will.

Oi, you hear me? Every bloody day!

She doesn't have to live with it.
I am left with the aftermath,

the debris, fixing cuts, wiping tears.
Holding Mum till she stops weeping.

A sound that chokes me.
I can take the shouts and screams,

but the weeping, the weeping paralyses me.
I step inside, quietly creep upstairs.

I feel guilty for not intervening.
I'm disgusted at my weakness.

What kind of woman do you want to become?
The words play around in my head.

Mum screams,
something breaks.

What kind of woman do you want to become?

I put a pillow over my head
and block out the sound.

CAN'T RELATE

I continue reading
about incredible
men and women
risking their own lives
for a better life.

Tonight it doesn't
ignite my fire.
Tonight it doesn't relate.

Tonight I feel
stupid.

Tonight I feel
useless.

Tonight I feel
foolish for thinking
we could ever

escape.

JOBCENTRE

The woman
tells me
to inform Dad
why the benefits
are all changing.

It's not really a cut.
It's all your benefits
in one lump sum.

But I don't get it
because there will be
less money than
we get now.

But her thin lips
say that it's pretty much
the same

and

*we just have to manage
our money better,*
she says,

looking at a
screen
and not
at us.

Can you manage that?
she asks.

She smells of cigarettes.
It's making me feel sick.
Her narrow eyes fix on me.

We can manage,
I say quietly.

She tells me she can refer us to
the money advice service,
to help with 'money management' and
does Dad want to sign up?

Are the classes in English?

At the moment, yes, she says.

Then no, I say.

So I can put down he's declined the referral?

Well . . . he can't speak English so he won't understand anything . . .

She rolls her eyes
while typing on the computer
and mumbling something
about checking with the council
and how they might do budgeting classes
for *our lot.*

She scribbles something on
a piece of paper
and I'm worried
I've said something wrong.

Is that alcohol I can smell on his breath?

I shrug my shoulders
and shake my head
at the same time.

I try and hold back tears
but my chin starts to wobble.

She looks at me with her small eyes.
She breathes on me with her cigarette breath.
She doesn't hide the thin-lipped smirk painted across her face.

NIKAME

Dad tells me
I'm useless.

He accuses me of
not translating properly

and,

**What's the point of school
if you can't do these basic things?**

If they're so basic, why can't you do them yourself?!

The words come out
without thinking.

His eyes are blood-red.
His face screwed up
like he's waiting to spit out
something rotten.

**I'll break every bone in your body,
don't think I won't,**
he hisses.

I stare back.
I'm terrified
but I
stare right back.

**Well, you have a dentist's appointment in two weeks
so you'll need me for that.**

I walk ahead,
not quite believing
what I just said.
I'm either really brave or
completely stupid.
I daren't look back.

I catch a glimpse
as I turn the corner
up the hill.
I see him standing,
staring at me.
Even from this distance
I can see his body is enraged.

TIRED

I copy Tara's maths homework during break.
Didn't get much homework done
after last night.

Dad came home super late
and used Mum as a punchbag,
for everything he hates about himself.

I yawn through classes.
Teachers telling me off,
especially Miss (Bitchy) Bates
in French class.

I'm sorry I'm boring you, Amber.
Maybe less TV and earlier nights in future.

The class sniggers.
Miss Bates looks pleased
with herself.

I want to stand up to her.
I want to say,
No, Miss, I'm not tired
because of watching TV till late.
I wish, Miss.
My dad hit my mum.
Bit difficult to sleep after that.
It's hard to sleep when you see your
mum get kicked or punched.
It's hard to dream after that, Miss.
I wish I was tired from watching
TV till late, Miss.
I really wish that was the case.

Instead all I can muster is,
Sorry, Miss.

FINAL SESSION

Last PE class before
half-term.
Before I start training
for the ESAC.

If I start training.
If I can find the courage.

WARM-UPS

High knees
side lunges
chest openers
shoulder rolls
wide squats
hamstring kicks

HIGH FIVES.

SUPERGLUE FAILS

The sole
of my trainer
comes unstuck.

Superglue
failing
its one
and only
job.

ONE HUNDRED METRES

On your marks,
get set,
GO!

No time to think.
No time for error.

Long strides.
No distractions.

Nought to sixty metres,
accelerate.

Sixty to ninety metres,
maximum velocity.

Ninety to one hundred,
power through to the finish.

Just before
I cross the line

something catches
under my foot

and I come crashing down,
burying chin in mud.

I look down at my feet
and see the sole of my trainer

almost completely detached.
I rip it off

as Sarah and Leanne
sprint finish to the end.

I get myself up
and limp to the finish line.

TOO TIRED TO RESIST

Miss Sutton
checks if I'm OK.

Time for a new pair of trainers,
she says.

Maybe it was the
meeting at the Jobcentre.
Maybe it was the fight last night.
Maybe I'm just too tired

because today
my secrets
are written all over my skin.

I'll sort something out, she says quietly.
Why don't you sit out for now?

I slump down on the bench,
frustration and embarrassment
playing ping-pong
in my head.

SELF-SABOTAGE

More selfies
and singing from
the cool girls
at the back of the bus.
And *Gemma*.

I mimic her voice.
Tara tells me to shush.

You really need to work on all of this frustration, you know.
It's bubbling up inside you and that can only lead to one thing.

She thinks for a moment.

It could be something to do with a past life.
My mum can do ancestral healing.
She did it on me and it turns out I was banished from a tribe
in Argentina like way back when. That's why I have issues with belonging.

Since when?
I say in a more
mocking tone
than I should.

Since always. You're not the only one with problems, you know.

Sorry.

It's fine.

She collapses back in her seat.
I feel guilty for all the
ugly thoughts
I've been having
about Tara.
There's not a bad bone
in her body.

I just can't help the jealousy
that eats away at my insides.
Once it takes over,
it's like I'm on a
fast train
to sabotage central,
determined to push
everyone away.

SCHOOL TOILETS

I stare at myself
in the mirrors.

Life is not a rehearsal.
What kind of woman do I want to be?
Beena's words still
running round my head.

And then *she* walks in.
Gemma Griffin.
I see her turn to leave
but it's too late.

She closes the cubicle door.

I wait.

Something rises inside me.
I walk to the door.
Bang on it with my fist.

Silence.

Fucking cow!

PRIDE

It doesn't make me feel good.
It churns me up inside,
but when that anger rises
it becomes a matter of pride.

MISS SUTTON

I charge out of the loo
and straight into Miss Sutton.

I have the letter I promised you.
Don't let me down –
the school needs you!

Yes, Miss, because it's THAT easy.

Miss Sutton looks at me.
Stunned.

My office, now.

Her voice sharp,
her eyes kind.

She sits me down.

What's going on?

We sit
in silence.

If you don't tell me, I can't help.

Her eyes are gentle.
She looks at me with kindness
and concern,
waiting for me
to tell her my truth.

TELL HER

Tell her I never sleep.
Tell her my life feels like a prison.
Tell her I wish I could run away.
Tell her I can't go against my dad.
Tell her the repercussions are worse than she could imagine.
Tell her I'm not really sure how long I can live like this.
Tell her I never feel safe.
Tell her.
Tell her.
Tell her.
Tell her.
Tell her.

I can't.
No matter
how much
I want to.

NOT TALKING

Secrets
are hands
round my throat.

The closer
I am to talking,
the tighter their grip.

THE LETTER

says

Dear Mr and Mrs Rai,

Amber is an extremely talented athlete and we feel she would be a real asset to the athletics team. Last year Amber stood out from the rest of the runners at the English Schools' Athletics Championships and caught the attention of sports officials. We all believe she has what it takes to go all the way. Many British Olympic athletes have come up through events like the ESAC and we can see Amber having a bright future in athletics.

Training will take place twice a week, starting after the autumn half-term, to be followed by several inter-school events as well as regional ones, and the UK under-seventeens county championships at the end of the school year, should she qualify.

It is a prestigious honour to be chosen for the schools athletics team. We are selective in our choice and only the very best students are picked.

Please do not hesitate to get in touch if you would like to discuss this further. Otherwise we are pleased to welcome Amber to the team and look forward to your presence at future athletics events.

Kindest regards,

Miss E. Sutton
Head of PE

A great letter.
It's just a pity
my parents will
never read it.

NEW TRAINERS

Before you go, Amber, these are for you.
I found them in lost property. I think they should fit.
Just until you get new ones. Or you could keep them –
they look hardly worn.

What if someone comes looking for them?

They won't. They've been in the box for years.

**Thanks, Miss. Just until my mum can buy new ones. I'll bring
them back.**

*Of course. But like I said they've been in the box years, so you
might as well keep them.*

I inspect them when I'm out of the office.
They look like new.
I marvel at the bright orange ticks.
I've never had a known brand of anything before.
One person's trash is another person's treasure
and I will certainly treasure these.

Nice Nikes! Wow, latest ones.
They cost a fortune!
Cool girl Bryony looks impressed.

Erm . . . I don't think they're the latest.

Trust me, I know my Nikes.
Good to see you're getting some style.

I look back at Miss Sutton's office.
Did she . . .
No, she wouldn't . . .
would she? . . .

THREE
CONTROL

ANATOMY OF A REVOLUTION STAGE 3

The rebels gain power.
The ruling regime
tries to suppress them
by any means
possible.

A NEW MAN?

I tremble,
my hand
unable to fit the key
in the lock.

Sitting at the kitchen table,
Dad looks at the clock,
pleased I've obeyed.

I try slipping upstairs
before he can engage.
His face softens.

Aren't you going to sit here and talk to me?

I've got homework to do.

Just five minutes. I'll make tea.

I'm confused –
this is new.

I have a test tomorrow,
I lie.

He looks down
with sad eyes
and nods his head.

OK.

The cord between his heart
and mine
tugs.

I see him as he was.
The dad that lifted me up
way above his head
and gently bopped my head
on the ceiling.

Half an hour, then.

Great, I'll make the tea.

His eyes light up.
He laughs.
I empty my bag of books,
spread them out on the kitchen table.
Start linking the stages
of a revolution to
modern-day revolts while
waiting for the comforting
aroma of cardamom
and fennel.

PERFECT

We talk
about making
chicken and rice
at the weekend.

Or do you want lamb?

Whatever you like, I say.

Whatever you like, he says.

**This week chicken,
next week lamb?
How does that sound?**

Great.

We'll make it together.

Perfect, I say.

Because this exchange is

PERFECT.

WAGES

Mum counts her meagre wages.

Don't tell your dad how much I got paid,
she says as she stuffs
a bundle of notes
down her
bra.

NEARLY HALF-TERM

The day before
half-term
we hang out at our
secret place.

Tara: Me and David were just talking about going to Birmingham
to check out the new arcade in StarCity,
maybe go to the cinema in the evening . . .
Do you think you can make it too?

I might be able to. Let me see.

Really? Oh cool!

I know I can't.
I have no money,
I can't risk being seen,
and out till the *evening*, yeah right!

So what day works for you both?

David shrugs.
It's up to you.

Yeah, whatever.

I try to sound casual
to hide the jealousy
twisting, worming its way inside.

Tuesday?

She's going to be alone with him!

Tuesday's good.

I feel sick.

Great, let's do that.
It's going to be so much fun!

Yeah, can't wait.

Tara. David. ALONE.

There's a pain in my chest
as neither of them realize
they're taking it in turns
to punch me right in the
HEART.

FAKE

I start listing
the reasons

in my head
as to why
Tara and I **S**houldn't
be friends.

Mayb**e**
this has a**l**ways
been **f**ake.

Maybe she stayed
to get clo**S**e
to David.

Maybe she's never
w**a**nted to be friends.

May**b**e she's a
big fat fake.

Maybe she wants it
t**o** be
the **t**wo of them?

M**a**ybe she's just
wantin**g** me out of the picture.

Maybe I'm gonna have
to start playing the gam**e**.

EMPTY GESTURES

Politics thrives on manipulation
and empty gestures!
Mr History Jones
jumps round the class excitedly.

It's all in the politician's character.
Look at what they do!
Not what they say!

On that note . . .
Lenin: hero or tyrant?

Everyone is silent
and for once
mine is the first and
only hand up.

SATURDAYS

Making chicken and rice
Dad's way.
Radio on, playing all
the latest Bollywood tunes
as we cook.

I can't remember the last time
we hung out like this.

He shows me how much
spice to add.

I do the famous taste test.

So good!
I say.

Just like this day.

JUBILANT

I sit in my room,
looking at the walls

and the uneven spaces
that have felt wrong
for so long.

I don't think.
I just do.

Pulling
pushing
tugging
throwing
cleaning
hoovering
Blu-tacking
fixing.

Until the whole room
is different.

Everything in a new place.
Filling in the gaps
left by Ruby.

Owning what is now mine,
because today
feels hopeful,
today feels new.

IGNORANCE IS BLISS

See no evil.

Dad danced while cooking.
I am not allowed to dance.
He has his own rules.

Hear no evil.

Here we are laughing.
He said he would break my bones.
I choose to forget.

Speak no evil.

I want to believe.
Today was real, not a dream.
He is a new man.

DISTRUST

Mum is surprised
Dad made the chicken.
She asks if he was

in a good mood –
and did he mind?

**Of course he didn't mind.
He was happy.**

Happy?
she says
in disbelief.

Like it won't last.
Like it wasn't real.

It annoys me.
I want her
to let him change.

I want to know
that it was real,
that it's here to stay.

BOTTLES

Mum wants me to help her,
but I'm not really helping.

I just sit and watch . . .
as she searches.

Under wardrobes,
under beds.

An old suitcase
reveals a hidden stash.

A half-bottle of Bacardi.
She holds it up.

This is your father.

She gives it to me
as she continues her searching.

The gap between a
chest of drawers and a wardrobe

reveals a bottle of whisky.
She holds it up.

This is your father.

She gives it to me.
The searching continues.

By the time we've turned the house over,
Mum has found seven bottles.

Whisky, Bacardi, rum, beer,
gin, vodka and more whisky.

This is your father.

She takes each one and
tips it down the sink.

Don't tell him.
Don't tell him what I've done.
Let's see, let's see what he does.

Her face awash
with confidence,

I admire her bravery,
but the last thing I want

is to witness
what he will do.

HALF-TERM

First day of half-term
and I'm on babysitting duty.

Mum's home early from the factory.
Something about an order not turning up.

She watches as I play with Tiya,
teaching her the alphabet.

Out of the corner of my eye

I notice Mum
pick up the books
once I'm done.

I notice her
flick through the pages,
trying to make sense of the letters.

I notice how
desperate she is
to know more, to WANT more.

MUM

A WOMAN'S LIFE

Pull through
get through
hold on
hold out
go on
keep on
carry on
stay around

remain alive.

A MEMORY

Thirteen.
A beating
that made
a cripple
out of me.

It never left.
The growth
may be gone
but the weight –
the weight
of it is
always
there.

A WOMAN LIKE ME

I was married at eighteen
to a man twenty years older.
Together we have two daughters.

People wonder why women like
me don't leave.
Where would I go?
No English, illiterate, no skills.

Where does a woman like that go?

I say I was cursed to have daughters,
not because
I don't want them
or love them –
it seems
the world doesn't want them,
or love them.

I want to save them
from the heartache of being
rejected, humiliated,
enslaved, voiceless.

I don't want them
to have my life.
I want more.
I see their potential and
it excites me and scares me.

How can I teach them
when I know so little myself?
How can I show them the way
when I myself have no map?

CHILDHOOD

I remember
walking to the market
to buy watermelons.
The biggest they've got,
my mother would say.
Rupi, my sister, and I would run,
race each other past
the Government High School,
looking at the girls
with blue and white ribbons in their braids
and boys with their
slicked-back oiled hair.
How we wished to be
one of those girls
behind those gates,
learning numbers,
reading books,
writing stories.

It's a hard life.
You have to accept it,
quietly endure your fate,
don't resist it.

Don't think,
don't feel,
because if you do
you'll want to change,
redraw the map,
rewrite the story,
and if you start thinking like that
and you're a girl . . .

God help you.

THE ARRIVAL

When I arrived in this country,
there were classes
I could have taken.

I could have learned to drive,
I could have learned to read and write.

But he couldn't read and write,
he didn't want a thinking wife,
a progressive wife,
a better life
for me,
for us.

The day after I arrived,
heavily pregnant,
he took me to the factory to start work.

I wake up at 5 a.m. every morning
Monday to Friday.
A flask of tea and a tiffin box
with last night's leftovers.

I leave at 6 a.m.

When my working day is done,
I lie on the kitchen settee.
Amber rubs my feet
and writes down my day's work
as I drift in and out of sleep.

Twelve hours a day,
dyeing jeans
for fancy West End shops,
with other women like me,
who have husbands like mine.
All breathing in the same poison.

I got so sick from the dye,
I remember lying on the living room floor,
emptying my guts.

The doctors said the blood tests
weren't 'normal'
and social services came to the house
wanting answers.

Where does your mummy go every day?
they asked Amber.

The shops,
she lied.
She only goes to the shops.

My boss was angry,
official people visited the factory,
and he said I had jeopardized the business.

My husband promised it wouldn't happen again,
pleaded with them to keep me on.

I have moved to sewing now.
I sew the jeans for the fancy West End shops.

GEMSTONES

They are in my heart.

My little Amber.
Firecracker.
So sick when born,
I tied an amber
gem on a string
around her tiny wrist.
I prayed
and prayed
and prayed.

The next day
it was like she was
never ill.

Amber,
a healing stone
for a healed child.

Ruby.
So much sadness.
The promise of a son
crushed.

I knew she needed
to grow up strong,
have fire to withstand
the walls built
round her.

The name Ruby seemed fitting.
An inner glow
so she might emit her
own light and
shine.

MY HUSBAND

Too tired to think,
too aching to protest.

I am up before my brain
has a chance to catch up,
before my body has time
to resist.

I roll out the chapattis
until he says
that's enough.

More often than not
I don't remember
how I ate,
how I changed,
how I got into bed.

A blur.

Before I know it,
I'm up again.
Filling up my tiffin box
and leaving for work.

This is not living.
This is surviving.

SPYING

From the kitchen window
I watch *The Man*
watering his rose bushes.

He looks in my direction.
I duck down under the window,
heart racing.

HELPLESS

Dad's back earlier than usual from the pub.
I've been trying to pluck up the courage
to tell him about athletics club,
but on a scale of one to ten
he's a twelve.

Look at her. Waste of space. Who'd want her?
Ruined my life. I drink because of her. She makes me do it,
he slurs.

Leave her alone.

My voice is weak.
I cower by the back door,
wanting to escape.

Then Mum starts crying.

I can't take it.
I can't take the sound.
It makes me want to vomit.

Stop it. Please, Mum. Stop it.
Shhhhhh.

I'm hugging her knees,
crouched on the floor,
angry.

Angry I can't help.
Angry I hide in corners.
Angry I'm too scared to raise my voice.
Angry I *can't* protect her.
Angry I *have* to protect her.
Angry I believed he'd changed.

ONE AND ONLY RULE

From now on,
look at what he does.
Not what he says.

Always
what
he
does.

MAKING SENSE

Ruby made sense of everything.
She made me feel safe.

Once you've seen the two people
that are supposed to take care of you

broken and beaten,
something changes inside you.

You don't feel safe.

You no longer sleep.
You're no longer in control

of what you feel
or what you think.

Everything ceases
to make sense.

DAD'S NIGHTMARES

At night,
he screams out for his mother.
We don't sleep.

At dinner,
he cries into his food.
We don't eat.

I want to hate him,
but when a grown man
screams out

for a parent
like a lost child,
that's hard to hate.

GROWING PAINS

I wonder if we ever grow up.
If some things are so painful,
we stay small on the inside.
Crying and screaming
but no one sees.

We just go about our normal business
like we're OK
and no one would ever know.

FIXING A PARENT

Can it be done?
Or are broken adults
too far gone?

TROUBLED SLEEP

Nightmares
engulf
dreams.

I'm buried
under the
rose bushes.

Clawing
Clawing
Clawing

       to

            get

                    out.

KEEPING THE DREAM ALIVE

Each day drags.
Each day the anxiety heightens
as I keep thinking
of every elaborate plan I can
so that I can do athletics.

I spend the week
playing tricks on myself.

Not knowing
means I can still live the fantasy.
The longer I put it off,
the longer the dream stays alive.

TELL THEM

Tell them.
Tell them.
Tell them.

I've been psyching
myself up
for hours.
Time is running out.

It's Sunday.
It's the end of half-term
and the first training session
is next week.

I could lie,
make up something
about a study group.

Or
I could tell the truth.

Always better to tell the truth,
I naively think.
Always better to tell the truth.

I do my
quiet kitchen dance.

Clear up
wash up
clean up
scuttle upstairs.

I sit.

Think.

On a scale of one to ten
he doesn't seem too bad.
Maybe a three.
Today is the day.

Scale of one to ten
my courage –
eight,
sliding down to a
         one
            with
               each
                  step
                    I
                      take
                        down
                          the
                            stairs.

DEEP BREATHS

I ask about tea,
I sit, I stand, I pace.

Something wrong?

I slowly find the words,
stuttering and stumbling out.

I said no!

Why not?

Because I say so.

That's not a good enough reason!

It's not right for a girl. You need to start behaving respectfully.

I take a breath.
Change tack.

I'm the most talented girl in school . . .

**You're too old to be gallivanting about and running round
a school field.**

Mum, what do you think?

It's up to your father.

But . . .

Are there boys at these events?

I don't know. No. What does it matter?!

**People will talk, that's why. 'We saw your daughter talking to
so-and-so, she was doing this, that and the other.'**

I'll just be running. That's all.

I've said no. Now, show some respect.

Why should I?! It's stupid! It's a stupid reason!

I try my best to be calm,
but I'm not very good at it.

I feel helpless and alone.
I run up the stairs,
into the bedroom,
and slam the door.

I want to throw things.
My heart is pounding
out of my chest.

I'm raging
so I'm crying.

I climb into bed,
pull the duvet over my head
and silently scream
into the darkness.

HOMEWORK

Trying to	write my truth.
Trying to	solve equations.
Trying to	figure out earthquakes.
Trying to	study the stages of a revolution.
Trying to	forget about athletics.
Trying to	forget about my dreams.

NUMB

Stopped   feeling
caring
loving
hating
thinking
speaking
sleeplng
liking
smiling
crying
dreaming
believing
wanting
living.

NOTHING TO SAY

David: That sucks.

I want him to hold me.

Tara: I'm so sorry, Amber.

She rubs my arm.
David keeps his hands in his pockets
and an ocean's distance between us.
He shares a look with Tara.
I stare at them both.
He sees I've seen it.
My jaw tightens.

I should go.

He fist bumps my shoulder and he leaves.

Is he annoyed with me?

Don't be silly.

I see in her eyes that she knows more
than she's letting on.

Do you need a hug?
You look like you need a hug.

I'm OK.

She squeezes me tight.
It feels great.
I sink into her shoulder,
wishing it were David's.

The whole world needs a shake and a hug right now, Amber.
The whole world.

THE ART OF REVOLUTION

History homework
is proving to be a good
substitute
for running.

Stories of revolts,
freedom fighters,
rebellions and their
rebels light a fire inside me.

Ordinary people
using their voice,
speaking out,
risking everything
to make a change,
gives me wings.

WHAT KIND OF WOMAN DO I WANT TO BECOME? 1

Downstairs
the shouting starts.
A glass breaks.

I stand,
my hand round
the doorknob.

Fear holds me back,
courage pushes
me forward.

I stand in the open doorway.
Another glass breaks
as I make my way

down the stairs.

WHAT KIND OF WOMAN DO I WANT TO BECOME? 2

Stop it,
I say too quietly.

Stop it.
A little louder.

Stop it.
Louder still.

Stop it!!
I scream.

WHAT KIND OF WOMAN DO I WANT TO BECOME? 3

Leave Mum alone!

A deep
strong
fierce
voice
rises
from
my
gut.

It sends
shockwaves
through
my father.

It builds
armour
round
my mother.

My father
steps
away.

He turns
to me.

**Don't ever raise your voice to me again.
I let it go once.
Next time you won't be so lucky.**

STORM

I am a hurricane.

Everything from the
night before
and beyond even that

is being whipped up inside me,
causing chaos,
stirring up every fear,

threatening to release
every secret.

I'm so angry
I can't see straight.
I can't see

until Gemma
and I
walk into each other.

I'VE GOT MY CROWD

We form a circle round her.

You're a stupid ugly bitch.
No one likes you.
No amount of make-up
can hide how ugly and disgusting you are!

I'm the leader.

And I
      spit
           in
                  her
                      face.

Everyone laughs.

I feel strong.
I feel powerful
as all my fears disappear.

LIKE FATHER LIKE...

I am
my father's
daughter.

TARA

You have to let things go with Gemma!

I hate her.

She said she was sorry for what she did.

She still walks around like she's IT.

You spat at her. That's not cool.

**You're right, it's not.
But how can you take her side?**

*I'm not. But you're so angry. Let's go to the toilets.
I'll teach you how to release negative emotions.*

**Oh my God, Tara, can you stop with this healing crap!
Leave me alone and go cuddle up with David.**

What?

**I have eyes, Tara. Don't deny it!
You're trying to push me out of the group.**

*We're your friends, Amber. Why can't you see that?
Why do you push everyone away?*

GEMMA

We were mates.

Then one day we had an argument
over an unfair tackle in netball.

We stopped speaking for two days
and in those two days
she told everyone
my dad was the drunk
who hung out
outside the shopping centre.

She called my mum the bag lady,
a tramp.
She said I was council-house scum.

My dad *is* the drunk outside the shopping centre.
I might be council-house scum.
However,
my mother IS NOT a tramp.

And that is why she deserves *everything* she gets.

A VISIT

When I come home
from school,
there is a young woman
sat in the kitchen
with Mum and Dad.

Dad sends me
to my bedroom.
I disobey the order
and sit on the stairs,
shuffling down,
one stair at a time
getting closer,
trying to hear her words.

She sits on the settee
in the kitchen,
head bowed, covered,
veil-like,
looking at her feet.

Coat on,
shoes off,
respectful but
not comfortable,
not staying long.

I think I recognize her
but I can't be sure.
She's looks familiar.
I try to remember
but I can't place
her face.

She talks to my parents.
Too quiet.
I'm on the bottom stair.
I peek round.
She's crying.

I see Mum give her a tissue.
She says something.
She's still too quiet.
My dad nods,
looking all important.

She keeps sniffing,
wiping her eyes.
Mum and Dad
don't say much,
just nod,
let her do the quiet talking
and crying.

No comfort.
Mum looks like
she wants to.

Silence.
Too long.
Uncomfortable.

Dad summons me.
I cautiously leave my place on the stairs
to join them in the kitchen.
I stand with my
back against the kitchen cabinets,
eyes wide, thinking,
It's her.

HARPREET 1

Harpreet, who ran away,
Harpreet, who ran away with a Bengali boy.
Harpreet, who was about to get married,
everything arranged,

but

she
chose

LOVE.

CHOOSING LOVE

I remember   being told she was bad.
I remember   being told she was the worst kind of girl.
I remember   being told she would have to run for the rest of her life.
I remember   being told she didn't love.
I remember   being told that choosing yourself was wrong.
I remember   being told that choosing for love is a sin.

I remember   feeling she was brave.
I remember   feeling she was right.
I remember   feeling I wanted her to win.
I remember   feeling happy for her.
I remember   feeling I'd do the same.
I remember   feeling I'd always choose love.

A LESSON

I stand with my back
pressed against the kitchen cabinets.

Dad tells me there is
something I need to hear.

An important lesson that needs
to be brought to my attention.

Dad sits.
Watching.
Watching me watching her.
I wait.
Impatiently patient.
Feeling the . . . watching.
Watching being watched.

Oh wow, you've grown so much.
Do you remember me?

I nod.

I've got something to say to you
and I want you to listen really carefully.

Can't you speak in Punjabi?
Dad barks.

It's easier in English, Uncle.
As you can tell, my Punjabi isn't great.
Forgive me.

She smiles
like she's an old friend.
But she's no friend.
I know what she's going to say
and I want to stuff my fist
in her mouth to stop her
vomiting any more words up.

The lesson starts.

A lesson in respecting our parents.

Don't do what I've done,
there was no love in my heart.

Thirty minutes of

shame shame shame shame,
ashamed ashamed ashamed ashamed,
respect shame respect shame,
don't don't don't don't,
shame shame shame shame,
a bit more respect,
a dash more ashamed,
sprinkle of shame,
and the icing . . .

It's not your life, it's your parents' life.

It didn't work out between her and him.
Love failed.
She crawled back to her parents
and now she's going to every relative's house
and begging forgiveness.

Don't ruin your life like I have.

Harpreet.
How dare she
snivel her way round every aunt and uncle,
helping to keep their daughters in check!

You don't want to end up like me.

Coming here grovelling,
making my life ten times worse,
filling it with fear
and keeping me on lockdown,
stopping my free thinking.

Have you told her? Dad asks.

A hint of suspicion in his voice,
bothered he hasn't understood
Harpreet's lecture.

Yes, Uncle, she says.

I want her to leave.
Spread her poison elsewhere.
The weight of her words
sits heavy inside me.
I feel branded,
chained,
suffocated.
My eyes sting,
there's something in my throat.
I'm beginning to feel the heat.
It starts in my back,
in the shoulder blades,
up my neck,
in my jaw,
a stinging behind the eyes,
in my hair,
down my arms,
hands into fists,
pulsing lungs,
a throbbing stomach.
I'm ready to pounce,
wanting to claw everyone to shreds.
Close my eyes:
keep it inside,
keep it inside.

Harpreet leaves and I am left.
Still standing
with my back against the kitchen cabinets.
Dad warns me:

You wouldn't be as lucky as Harpreet.
You wouldn't be accepted back.

You're old enough now.

He points at me.

**You need to start behaving,
and there are rules.**

HARPREET 2

Harpreet is

A warning

Representative of

Patriarchal

Rules

Ending freedom

Establishing a

Tight rein.

FOUR
MOMENTUM

ANATOMY OF
A REVOLUTION
STAGE 4

Revolutionaries gain
allies.

Support for a rebellion
spreads.

It's almost
time.

STUDENT-TEACHER

I sit with Tiya.
Start teaching her the alphabet.
When she's bored, preferring
the red truck to her book,
Mum picks up the book.
I watch her turn the pages,
her eyes absorbing the
brightly coloured pictures.
Her face yearning . . .

Teach me,
she says.

TEACH ME

Mum picks up my history book.
The Art of Revolution.

Teach me to read this.

This is too hard.
One day, in the future.
Let's start with this.

I pick up Tiya's ABC book.
I place it open in front of us.

Let's start with the alphabet.

And we start going through it.
Letter by letter.

She stops at F.

Don't tell your father.

ALLIES

Me
and
Mum.

There's a fire in

her

that's even stronger than

mine.

X MARKS THE SPOT

I sign Amber's letter.
I sign it, setting her free.
I sign it,
sealing my fate.

Mum signs my letter,
setting me free.
She signs it
and we are rebels planning to rebel.

THE ANATOMY OF A REBEL

Qualities of a successful revolutionary.
History homework.

Seek liberation.
        (Teach Mum to become literate.)

Hold on to your vision.
        (Being free of Dad.)

Act on gut instinct.
        (Mum and I can outsmart Dad.)

Stay focused.
        (We can't give up on our dream.)

Navigate the hurdles.
        (Dad will try and stop us.)

Break all the rules.
        (Keep going regardless.)

Lift others as you rise.
        (Me and Mum, together.)

BUTTERFLIES

I race up and
down the fourteen stairs
in our house.

Stomach feeling too
fluttery to eat breakfast.

Feel like our secret –
mine and Mum's –
is bursting
out of me.

Like it's obvious
to him,
to everyone.

I try and act normal.
Drink my tea
all normal
and have a piece
of toast
all normal.

What's wrong with you?
he asks.

Nothing.

You're acting strange.

He seems grumpier than usual.

I have a test today.

Make my breakfast.

I jump up,
not wanting to
create any more
suspicion.

Pour some cereal
in a bowl,
add milk and
place it on the table.

**Don't do that stupid
running up and down the stairs.
You woke me up.**

Sorry. I'll be quieter next time.

There won't be a next time.

His head looks like it
might drop into the bowl
of cornflakes.

He gets up from the table,
takes a bottle of whisky
from underneath
the kitchen worktop.

He pours a shot
into his cereal.

Medicine,
he says
and chuckles.
Stops the shaking.

He mixes it into the milk,
lifts the bowl up to his lips
and gulps it down
like it's a pint
of beer.

LEAVING THE ESTATE

is like leaving
a concrete
prison.

The high-rises
weighing down on you
like giant watchtowers
with spying eyes
in every direction.

I see *The Man.*
He puts two
bags of rubbish
into his bin.

Rubbish bags full of what?

I have visions of
body parts
and feel sick
to my stomach.

Hi! he says

I freeze,
stare at his face,
unable to move or speak.

You OK?

I think I nod.

How are your parents?

I'm frozen to the spot.

OK. You have a good day.
Are you sure you're OK?

I think I nod.

I turn, I run.
I run so fast.
As fast as I can.
I imagine Ruby next to me.
I imagine her holding my hand
as I squeeze the air with my fist.

THE WEIGHT OF A SECRET

My bag is heavy with the signed letter
burning through my shoulders
as I enter the school
gates.

I make my way
to Miss Sutton's
office.

Miss!

I hold in my
mix of emotions –
fear, excitement,
fear.

I take the letter from my bag
and hand it over.
Signed.

This is fabulous news!
I'm so happy they came around.

Yeah.

See you tomorrow for our first training session!

Can't wait.

The letter still
leaving a ghost-like weight
on my shoulders
as I make my way to class.

HISTORY

We learn
what makes a
successful revolution.

One.
It takes time
and organization.

Two.
Entrenched regimes
do not leave
quietly.
Be prepared to keep
fighting.

Three.
Strikes are key
to gaining psychological power.

Stand your ground.

Breathe,
something whispers.
Stay strong.
Fight.
All in good time.

TUCK SHOP

The bell is a signal for me, not for you!

Mr History Jones
shouts as we quickly
pack away our books
and head out for break
as fast as we can.

I meet Tara and David
by the football pitch.

Tuck shop?
I'll go, it's my treat.
My gran gave me some money
over half-term for putting up her curtains.

I'll come with you!

And before I can
suggest that we all go together,
Tara and David are linking arms
and walking quickly to
the tuck shop,
whispering.

I almost follow,
but I get the feeling
they want to be alone.
The whispering and
the closeness between them
as they walk suggests
something must have happened
over half-term.

I feel overwhelmed by anger
and consumed by heartache
all at the same time.

I wait impatiently
for them to come back.

When I see them
walking towards me,
they're deep
in secret talk.

There you are, your fave.

David drops
a Twix into my lap.

Thanks for running off.

Sorry, my fault. I wanted to get there before the rush.

The lie from Tara's lips
is so obvious.

I find myself
breathing deep,
trying to swallow my frustration
while we make fun of the
cool girls
hanging out with
the cool boys
on the football pitch,
screaming every time
a ball comes hurtling towards them.

SCHOOL TOILETS

Our school toilets
are the worst.

Graffiti on every door
and questionable stains
on the tiles.

As Tara and I enter,
we see Gemma
fixing her eyeliner
with Nicola and Sandy.

They shield her
like I'm a tornado
and she needs protection
from being swept
up and away.

It's like everyone
is holding their breath.

In a world where I
feel like no one,
it's a strange kind of power
that makes me feel like
someone.

THE QUIET RUSH

Rush, rush, rushing,
with precision.
Keeping it quiet,
keeping it calm.

Ruby is here
with Jas
and Tiya.

Rush, rush, rushing,
making sure
Dad doesn't need to ask twice,
making sure my brother-in-law
has everything he needs.

Keeping it calm,
keeping it quiet.

We serve.
They eat first.
The men always eat first.

When they finish eating,
they retire to the living room
to drink whisky.

I serve Bombay mix
and crisps,
whatever Dad requests.

When they are done drinking
in the living room,
they go to the pub.

That's when we eat.
That's when we talk
louder than a whisper.

ALL IN GOOD TIME

The only thing
that keeps me going
is athletics.

Knowing I'm
starting training
tomorrow,

knowing I might
make it to the
county championships.

Knowing training
means two extra
evenings with David

means I can
and will
put up

with the quiet
rush, rush,
rushing.

THE FIRST SESSION

Miss Sutton's pep talk.

This is only the beginning.
We have a long road ahead.
This right here is what matters.
How hard you work now
will determine how well you all do in the competitions.
So give it your all in these sessions.
This is YOUR time.
Your time is NOW.

I feel high with excitement.
David's sitting next to me.

So glad you're here,
he says.

Me too.

And he swings his arm
round my shoulder
and gives me a
hug in a headlock.

I can't stop smiling all
the way to
King Edward's sports field.

HILLS 1

Miss Sutton says:
Hill training will be hard.
You might even feel like you're going to pass out!
But trust me,
hill training will make you stronger!

Everyone is commenting
on my Nikes.
Embarrassment trickling through
pride.

They fit OK?
Miss Sutton whispers.

Yes. Thanks, Miss.

Excellent.

She gives my shoulder
a tap and a squeeze.

I jog to the bottom
of the hill.

I look up at Miss Sutton
shouting instructions.
I look down at my feet,
at my new not-old,
definitely-not-lost-property trainers,
feeling grateful,
feeling strong,
feeling I might really

fly.

HILLS 2

Focus on running tall.
Head, shoulders, hips
and ankles aligned.

Look ahead
short strides
pump arms
lift knees
run tall.

Looking ahead
running tall.

Looking ahead
pumping arms
lifting knees
running tall.

Looking ahead
running tall.

Pump
lift
run
look.

Look   ahead.

Looking   ahead.

Till I reach the   top.

MINIBUS POLITICS 2

No politics in this group.
We are equals.

Right here and now
I feel like I belong.
A sense of belonging
I've not felt
in a long time.

This is family.

GIDDY

David and I take selfies
on the minibus.
Just silly ones.

That's what I like about you –
you're not like other girls,
he says.

My head's been
swimming
ever since.

RESTRICTIONS

My walk home
goes from open
skies
to watchful
eyes
as I enter
my estate.

SITTING IN MY ROOM

Trying to do homework,
but all I can think about is David.
Imagining what it would
be like to hold hands,
what it would be like
to kiss him.

Wondering
if he's already
kissed Tara.

DISGUISE

Dad sits on my bed.

People tell me things,
he says.
His voice is calm.
His face soft.

There are people everywhere that know us.
You can't do things that would bring shame on us.

I'm not.

I don't want to say you can't do this and you can't do that.
I'm just trying to do my best. I'm trying to protect you.
Do you understand what I'm saying?

Yes.

Good. As long as you know that.
People tell me things.

I know.

So you were just at school doing extra study?

Yes.

That's OK then, if that's the truth.
I just care. That's all.

When he leaves,
I start shaking.
I can't make sense
of it.

My heart says
he cares,
he just cares,
bogged down by
pressure outside *his* control.

My mind says,
One and only rule:
look at what he does,
not what he says.

NO FEAR

I see
everything.
I'm standing
my ground
as Dad
tries **so** hard
to keep
us under
his thumb.
We will not
be **scared** into
surrender.
We will not
lose momentum.

FIVE
HONEYMOON

ANATOMY OF A REVOLUTION STAGE 5

Revolutionaries
gain power.

But –
honeymoons
never
last.

MUM'S HOME

I write her day's work
in her little book.

When Dad leaves for the pub,
she asks,
Did you go?

Yes, but I think he might know.

Shhh,
she says.

Don't worry.
I'll handle it.
Happy?

I nod fiercely.

Happy.

DAD'S BACK 2

Turn the volume down,
turn the telly off.
Don't say a word.
Can't he wait?
Five minutes,
just five minutes.

He stands in the doorway,
swaying.
Mum – exhausted – rolls out chapattis.
I serve.

Dad first,
he always eats first.

One day
this will change.

Must   be   patient.
All   in   good   time.

BECOMING LITERATE

When *he* goes to bed,
and we hear *him* snore,
her lesson starts.

Tiya's box of books
is a treasure trove
of learning for Mum.

LESSONS

The alphabet.

I write a letter
on each piece of paper.
I lay them out on the floor
like a giant poster.
She has almost got it
by heart.

I mix the letters.
She's quick to learn.

I recall Miss Sutton's pep talk.

This is only the beginning.
It's a long road ahead.
This is *her* time.
Her time is NOW.

FIRST WORDS

Mm ah tt	MAT	**Listening**
Ss ah tt	SAT	**to**
Buh ah tt	BAT	**her**
Buh oo tt	BOOT	**sound**
Buh ih tt	BIT	**out**
Ff uh nn	FUN	**words**
Tt ee ch	TEACH	**is**
Luh uh vuh	LOVE	**beautiful.**

HOPEFUL

It feels like things are
possible.

Dad's nightmares
are drowned
by dreams
of the good life.

A life where
Mum and I
live with open skies
without towers
and concrete.

Where Ruby and I
laugh like we used to.
Love like we used to.

Space to breathe
Space to run.

                    Space to fly.

LIFE

It's shifting

and something
inside is

lifting.

GAMES

I'm busy rattling my tongue off,
trying to make David laugh.

Me and Tara,
playing games,
trying to keep David's attention.

I see it
even if she thinks
I don't.

He seems to be mesmerized
when she twirls her hair.

So I tell another joke,
make him laugh.

Tara giggles,
using the excuse to
touch his arm.

EQUATIONS

I sit enraged
in maths.

Working on
simultaneous equations.

If $x = Tara$
and $y = David$,

what is the probability
they are in love?

Answer:
very likely.

WHAT WOULD HE EVER SEE IN ME?

Tara is   stunning
                        perfect
                        petite
                        girly
                        nice
                        kind
                        generous
                        clever.

I am
I am
I am
I am

                        nothing.

We don't compare.
It's not like the running track.
In this game,
I'm so far behind
I'm a dot
on the horizon
to them.

TRAINING

High knees
hamstring curls
jog round the field.

Our first competition is
coming up after Christmas.

Miss Sutton gives
us another pep talk.

You need to start thinking of yourselves as a team.
Not individuals. During the inter-school games
we stick together, lift each other, are there for each other.
We win together.
This is more than our own individual sports.

The team high-fives.
David catches my hand,
holds it in a fist.
I try and pull away.

Hey, what's up?

Nothing.

I want to ask him about Tara.
I want to know why he can't just tell me.

Hey, sister from another mister . . .

Don't call me that.

Whoa, what's going on?

Please, I just want to focus.

Are we OK? You've been acting strange.

Of course we are,
I lie.

I turn, start jogging,
hoping each stride
will shake out the
jealousy raging inside.

HIGH SPIRITS

Getting off the school bus,
I forget myself for a moment.
Runner's high
has me letting my guard down.

I forget about Tara and David.
What does it matter?
It's not like we could ever date.
Just be friends,
be grateful that we're friends,
I tell myself.

Outside the gates
I hug David goodbye.

I'm sorry I've been weird.

He takes my arms away
and steps back,
holding me at arm's length.

Easy. Do you think it's safe to do that?

Of course, don't be silly.

I fling my arms round him.
Just as we embrace,
a car whizzes by
and from the car window
someone looks me

dead
in
the
eye.

PANIC 1

I feel like I'm choking.
I let go of David,
push him away,
run into school
with David running after.

What's going on?

Someone saw.
Someone saw.

My breath is shallow,
my legs collapsing
underneath me.

Who? What?

I'm gonna get killed.
He's gonna kill me.

Who? Look at me. Calm down.

I'm on my knees,
the world is spinning,
David's voice is an echo.

Leave me alone.
Stay away.
You have to stay away.

Somehow –
I don't know how –
I run home.

PANIC 2

I check his face
for clues.

The phone rings.
I jump
out of my skin.

I run upstairs,
vomit into the toilet.

I lie on my bed,
wishing the ground
would swallow
me up.

PANIC 3

It's been weeks.
Dad hasn't said anything
about anyone seeing me
hugging David.

Still

I'm not sure how much longer
I can keep up the lie
about training being a study group.

Every time I'm on the sports field
running,
I'm haunted by the words:

'You know the man across the road . . .'
Should we shame, dishonour or disobey,
we would end up the very same way.

DISTANCE 1

No more
headlocks
wrist holding
hand grazing
arm round my shoulder
arm round my waist.

Instead, he walks ahead,
only I haven't asked him to.

DISTANCE 2

Weeks pass as
David and I
drift further apart
and he and Tara
float closer together.

ANXIETY 1

I tell Mum
that I
think he knows,
that I
can't keep going
with the lie,
that I
feel sick with worry.

Mum is calm.

We make plans.
We hide evidence.
We get our story straight.

RUBY'S TRICK 2

The teaching stops
with a knock at the door.

Both of us thinking it's
Dad, too drunk to find his keys.

We hide all the evidence
under the settee.

I sneak a peek
out of the window.

It's Ruby and Tiya.
Mum relaxes. I am tense.

Once they're inside we continue our lesson.
Ruby sits silently, Tiya bouncing on her knee.

Mum reads one of Tiya's alphabet books out loud.
I give her a little help when she's stuck on a word.

Wow, Mum, that's amazing.

I still needed your help.

Not on all the letters.

Mum looks pleased with herself.

Was I good?
she asks Ruby.

Ruby nods.
Really brilliant, Mum.

She pretend-yawns.
Pretends to rub her eyes.
Fingertips to sockets,
trying to fool me
with her Ruby trick.

RUBY

FAILED ATTEMPT

I ran away once.
I ran out of the house.
No shoes, no jacket,

in the middle of December,
a light covering of snow
on the ground.

I didn't even make it round the corner
before my dad grabbed my hair

and pulled me back inside.
I screamed the estate down.

Curtains twitched
but everyone stayed inside.

X, Y AND Z

I was set
to achieve all my dreams.
University, studying
journalism.

Straight As in GCSEs,
straight As in A levels.
My picture in the local paper.

Working-class girl
done good.
I was exceptional.

Then Dad got mad.

Someone, somewhere,
had told him that
girls do
x, y, z
at university.

That so-and-so's daughter
did
x, y, z
and now

she's run away,
got pregnant,
doing drugs.

He was told,
you need to hold on
to your daughters,
keep them close.

And that was that.

Dad thought it best
I get married
and there was no one
to stop it.

I tried,
but In the end
I wasn't strong enough.

AMBER

Just because	I can't talk to her
doesn't mean	I don't love her
doesn't mean	I don't want her
doesn't mean	I don't want the old days back
doesn't mean	I don't want to hold her
doesn't mean	I don't care about her
doesn't mean	I don't worry about her
doesn't mean	I don't want the best for her
doesn't mean	I don't want to protect her
doesn't mean	I want her life to turn out like mine
doesn't mean	I don't want her to fly
doesn't mean	I'm unaware of how mean I am
doesn't mean	I don't know what I've said and done
doesn't mean	I don't want to make it right
doesn't mean	I don't think about her EVERY DAY
doesn't mean	that my heart doesn't ache for losing her
doesn't mean	I don't know that I'm the one to blame.

TIYA

I am not a natural mother.
This I know.

I did things in the order I thought I should.
I thought a baby would give me

something to love.
A reason to stay.

But there is a switch inside
that hasn't been turned on –

or maybe it's been switched off?
It's difficult to know

which way round it happened.

JAS

We met twice before the wedding, with our families.
First on the 20th of April. Again on the 5th of May.

We agreed to be married on the 6th of May
and were wed on the 19th of June.

We were, are, strangers.

The only thing I know for sure is that he is kind.
He is the best father to Tiya.

When the family hoped for a boy,
he put his hand on my stomach and whispered

that he wished for a girl.

Marriage first, love second.
You learn to love, they say.

It works. For so many people it works.
But I feel my heart is locked.

When love has not been in abundance,
you seek it first.

You look for it in every corner of your being.

Love.

Love must always come first.

THEY SAY

I'm like Mum,
her personality,
her looks.

They say

I am delicate,
I am just like a flower,
like a quiet little mouse.

They say

I am all my mum.
I'm nothing like Dad.
Little do they know.

CHRISTMAS HOLIDAYS

As if it were even possible,
he drinks more at
this time of year.

HOMEWORK

I immerse myself
in revolutions
and rebels
as wars rage
in my home.

LESSONS CONTINUE

I hold up an
A4 piece of paper.

Not 'O' . . .
Look at the straight line.
No?
D.

Mum is doing great
but some letters still confuse her.
I pick up another A4 piece of paper.

This is O,
this is D –
see the difference?
D has a straight line.
O. D.

I shuffle the paper.

Which is O and which is D?

She points to the correct letter.

. . . Good.

SIX

TERROR

ANATOMY OF A REVOLUTION STAGE 6

Using terror
to maintain
control.

Your loyalty and
your strength
are tested.

No
one
is
safe.

DAD'S BACK 3

Turn the volume down,
turn the telly off.
Don't say a word.
Can't he wait?
Five minutes,
just five minutes.
He stands in the doorway,
swaying.

Mum – exhausted –
rolls out chapattis.
I offer to make them,
but Dad wants Mum to make them.
Mine won't be good enough.

I serve.

Dad eats.

Everyone is quiet.

THE ARGUMENT

Dad: These chapattis are dry.

Mum: It's yesterday's dough.

Why are you serving me bad food? You trying to kill me?

It's not bad. Just not fresh. It's from yesterday.

You trying to make me ill?

Let me butter them.

You think I'm going to eat them?

I'll make new dough.

So I can sit and watch the rest of my food go cold?

I'll put it back in the pot.

**Are you stupid? Are you? Are you brain-damaged?
What is this crap?**

THE FIGHT

Hot food on my arm.
Mess on the carpet.
Blood on Mum's head.

Mum running.
Kitchen to hallway to lounge.
Dad cutting her off,
Mum turning.
Lounge hallway kitchen stairs.
Dad is faster,
me running behind them,
trying to get between them.
Mum and Dad's room.
Mum gets a suitcase.
He pushes her against the wardrobe.

So you want to leave me? You want to leave me?

Banging on the front door.

Everyone. Is. Quiet.

THE TRIGGER

Mum is being carried out
on a stretcher.

Our neighbour is standing outside
with a cup of tea.

He's really gone and done it this time.
I'm keeping quiet,
but you, my girl, wanna
save yourself.

HOSPITAL

Hope is lost. Thoughts

Of ever being free

Seem so far away.

Palpitations of anxiety

Inducing feelings

That turn my stomach upside down

As I watch my mother sleep,

Looking like a vulnerable child.

HOME FROM HOSPITAL

I make her comfy on the sofa
and take the day off from school.
I try and form a protective
shield around her tiny 4 foot 11 frame.
I feel if I'm around her all the time,
he can't get near.

Let her heal this time.

I want to make her happy.
Place a light bulb in
every dark thought,
charge her up,
give her courage
to leave, something, anything.

OUR CHRISTMAS

isn't
like
anyone
else's.

HOLIDAY TRAINING

requires some
imagination.

I offer to go to the shops
whenever I can.

Work on my sprints
down to the petrol station.

Work on my hills
on the way back up.

I continue with my lunges
and squats and burpees.

I need to stay strong.
I add more press-ups

to my routine.
I do bicep curls

with shopping bags full of tins
and triceps dips on the kitchen chair.

Something tells me my arms need to be
just as strong as my legs.

THE BIG CHRISTMAS SHOP

This used to be Ruby's domain
and without her
I'm lost.

No fun bingeing
on your own.

Mum and I
walk down the sweets aisle
in the supermarket.

Have whatever you like.
Whatever's going to make Christmas good for you.

I don't know.
I don't need anything.

She picks up a bottle
of pink lemonade,
wincing with pain.

You like this?

Yeah.

Put it in the basket.

The first time we bought pink lemonade
Ruby and I pretended it was
champagne.
We drank it all on Christmas Day,
got ourselves drunk on sugar.

Put it in the basket,
she says again.

We're going to have the best Christmas ever.
You'll see.

PROGRESS

She takes the paper and
moves it close to her face,
then far away,
then close.
I want to laugh
but don't want to put her off learning.

S.

Good.

She takes the next piece of paper
She looks at me,
then at the paper.

**It doesn't matter if you don't know the word.
Can you make out the letters?**

She studies it.
Again, moving the paper close to her face
and then further away.

This one says Rai.

It does,
she's right,
but I think it's a lucky guess,
so I ask her to read out the letters.
She does the same dance,
close, far, close, far,
then she turns the paper upside down
and cocks her head to the side.
She's confused
so I turn the paper the right way up.

What's this letter?

Her mouth opens; nothing.

This one?

Mouth opens; nothing.

I know it says Rai, I just don't know the letters,
she says.

That's OK, we'll keep going through it.

And we do.
Over and over and over
again.

CHRISTMAS DAY

Mum and I
alone
all
day.

Eating.
Chatting.
Watching
TV.

When Dad
stumbles in
after midnight
he collapses
on the settee
and falls asleep.

The day
comes and goes
without a
fight or
beating.

Mum was right.
We have had the best Christmas ever.

SECRET STASH

I put away clothes
into drawers.
I notice a bundle of papers
under Mum's underwear.

Scraps and scraps of paper
with her name
written on all of them.
Some right.
Some wrong.

One perfect.

MRS SURINDER RAI.

SUNDAYS

Temple.
I usually make excuses,
I try to avoid it.

Homework,
exams,
feeling sick.

Tomorrow
is New Year's Day.
I can't get out
of this one.

Dad insists
we need to cleanse ourselves
of past sins and
pray for a better year.

I hate to tell him, but
no amount of praying
will cleanse him
of his sins.

AUNTIES AT THE TEMPLE

I am   asked where I've been.

I am   told it's been too long.

I am   asked my age seven times.

I am   asked if I'm considering university. When I say *yes,*

I am   met with annoyed looks.

I am   told there's no point.

I am   told it's too expensive.

I am   told it's best to settle down.

I am   told to make my parents happy. When I say I'm too young,

I am   told engagements can last a long time and there's no hurry.

I am   laughing in my head because no one can see the irony.

I am   told to give their condolences to Ruby for having a girl.

I am   told how tall I've got.

I am   told I'm the opposite to Ruby, who is just like Mum.

I am   told I am just like Dad, that I have his height.

I am   trying to contest it. I don't like being told

I am   anything like Dad.

RESPECT

Dad sits at the top
of a long table,
like a kingpin
in a gangster movie.

The other uncles greet him.
They shake his hand.
He is fawned over
and is well respected.

I watch Mum
still afflicted with pain
as she sits
with her tray of food.
She still needs painkillers,
she still can't sleep on her side,
she is walking with a limp.

He is seen as
a pillar of the community,
a righteous man,
a holy man.

It is time someone
knocked
him
off
his
throne.

WRITING

Ruby and Tiya
are here to see in
the new year.

I wish she'd spent it with
Jas and her in-laws.
I promise myself

I'll
be
nice.

Before Dad comes back,
I tell them to sit down
around Mum
at the kitchen table.

I give Mum a pen and paper
and we all watch her
write her name.

It's a moment
of monumental

significance.

NEW YEAR

Tesco's Finest chocolate eclairs.
I've been staring at them all week.
Mum complaining I'd break the freezer

if I kept opening and closing the door.
They've been defrosting for
nearly twenty-four hours in the fridge.

Spongy fingers
filled with cream,
topped with dark chocolate.

French, fancy, posh, a treat.
We are none of these things,

but it's a treat for New Year.
The best yet.
The fanciest New Year yet.

For one night we can transform.
Pink lemonade at the stroke of midnight
and then the eclairs.

I figure if I begin the new year eating something that good,
something that's the opposite of us,
it'll really be the start of new things.

Are they defrosted yet?

They will be by tonight.

Mum getting annoyed
with me opening the fridge
every half an hour.

After dinner, Dad's out down the pub.
Ruby and I tell him to come back early.
Eleven thirty, we say, so we can watch the fireworks on the telly.

Don't be late!
Otherwise you won't get an eclair
and we'll drink all the pink lemonade.

We all joke, but I know
we all have a knot
in our stomachs.

We watch the countdown to the
one hundred greatest comedians
with one eye on the clock.

Eleven thirty.

Take the eclairs out of the fridge,
place them on a large dinner plate
in the style of a fan.

I give them a sniff. Sweet.
We flick between watching fireworks
in Sydney, Bangkok and

ninety-four on the greatest comedians list.
All the time looking at the door,
occasionally thinking we can hear a key being turned.

Twelve thirty.

Still waiting.

One a.m.

Still waiting.

Mum tells us to call the hospitals.
A yearly ritual.
Same for the past four years.

Last year it wasn't a waste of time.
He'd been found in the street.
Soaked by the rain.

Unconscious, passed out.
Paramedics thought he'd been there for hours.
A week in hospital with a bout of pneumonia.

No one of his description in the local hospital tonight.
We pour the lemonade down the sink
and throw the untouched eclairs in the bin.

Two thirty.

There's a knock at the door.
It's our neighbours.
They're holding Dad.

We found him at the top of the road.

The boy goes to my school,
he's in sixth form.
He gives me a sympathetic smile.

I am mortified.
Dad's drooling and mumbling some crap.
He's too big and heavy,

but they manage to lay him
on the floor in the living room.
There's a stain on his trousers and a horrible smell.

We tell Mum not to touch him,
to let him wake up in the morning
and see what he's done for himself.

But she doesn't listen.
Says he'll ruin the carpet,
and quietly and obediently does her duty.

None of us can pick him up
so he's going to have to stay on the floor,
ruining our New Year and the carpet.

Mum is in the kitchen,
putting the washing machine on.
Ruby and I stand and look at him.

I hate him, she says.

Then she kicks him.
Right in the thigh.
He groans a little.

What are you doing?!

Why not?
He ruins everything.

She runs upstairs.
I am left on my own.
Standing,

staring at this mess of a man.
This massive embarrassment.
I hear Mum coming in from the kitchen

and, before she does,
I whack him on the ankle.

That's for the eclairs.

And leg it upstairs.

THAT NIGHT

Ruby and I talk.
So many things
that had been left unsaid
now pouring out
like the concrete
used to build the towers
that loom over us.

TWO SIDES TO EVERY STORY

RUBY

When I was told to get married,
I fought.
Believe me, I fought.
You weren't always there.
You didn't see it all.
I had to think what was best for you.
I had to protect you.
I distanced myself
because I needed to survive.
I've been in survival mode
ever since.
Yes, I get angry
because I don't know
how else to cope.

I thought you hated me.

What?

AMBER

It felt like you gave up.
It's been so hard on my own.
I can't stop the fights.
No one is here.
You don't see it now.
I tried talking to you.
I wanted to protect you.
I've been so lonely.
I've missed you so much.
I couldn't understand
what I'd done wrong.
Yes, I get angry
because it's easier
to cope with the pain.

I thought you hated me.

What?

LOVE

What has been
buried
for so long
finally comes

leaping   out.

LIKE OLD TIMES

Mum joins us.
The three of us huddle together
in my bed.

Nestled into the warmth
and protection of
each other's bodies.

THE MORNING AFTER THE NIGHT BEFORE

I'm in charge of the keys.
I'm not to let him out.
Not to tell him where the keys are.
Not to tell him where all his booze has gone.
Mum's given me this responsibility.
Made me promise.
I wish she hadn't.
It makes me nervous.
He's unpredictable.
I hope he stays asleep till she comes back.
It's not something I want to be dealing with.
But he doesn't stay asleep.
He's up and looking in all the cupboards.
He's turning the place over
and I'm hiding,
trying to stay small.
He finds me,
stands in front of me, shaking.

Where is it?
he says.

I act dumb.
What?

You know what. My medicine.

He says he knows I'm lying.
Says he knows it's in the shed.
I tell him I don't have the key,
lie and say Mum took it with her.
He's telling me the booze isn't bad,
it's medicine.
I'm saying I'm under strict instructions
not to let him out into the garden.
He's pleading.

I'm pleading.

I'm gonna get in trouble.

You won't, I promise.

I will.

I'll say that I found the keys.

I'll get in trouble.

We're both crying
and he's on the floor
on his knees
in front of me,
begging.

Please ... please ...

I reach into my pocket
and hand over the keys.

FINAL LESSONS

I have been teaching
Mum every evening
for the past four months.

You should go to the community centre, Mum.
They have language courses there.
They could teach you better than me.

She remains silent as
I watch her copy out
simple sentences.

BACK AT SCHOOL

I hand in my history
assignment.

Revolutions,
triggers
and wars.

I hand in my
English essay,
devoid of truth.

An essay of lies,
of perfect Christmases
and New Year celebrations.

STRANGERS

I sit with them.
We don't speak.

I become invisible,
sitting in the library at lunch,

reading up on how
revolutions fail when groups split.

They ask if I'm OK. I shrug.
They link arms with me. I push them away.

They ask me to hang.
I make my excuses.

Yet we are strangely
still a three.

LYING

If I asked you to lie for me, would you?

Mum is looking at me,
serious,
her brow furrowed,
her eyes anxious.

Yeah. Why?

I want to do an evening course.
In English, like you suggested.
I saw that lady Beena in town.
She said she can teach me now.

I know
she isn't telling me
the truth.

I know
Beena doesn't teach
the English class.

I know
Beena helps women
leave their husbands.

AN·XIETY 2

I feel like
I'm in the ocean
adrift, all alone,
and all the bits
and pieces that
make me who I
am are floating
all around me
and I'm trying
to grab them,
but every time
I get close
a wave comes
and washes them
further away.

DAD

Is there more
to   him?

The   animal
The   beast
The   wife-beater
The   alcoholic
The   threat
The   monster
The   man
The   husband

My   father?

NOT READY FOR CHANGE

I need
to believe
there is.

There is
more
to him.

I need
to believe
because

I thought
this was
what I
wanted.

But now
leaving
scares me
more than
staying.

MAKING PLANS

Mum has me looking at
important documents in folders.

Anything with her name on.

She doesn't tell me why,
just that she needs them.

WHEN

life
feels
like

it's
out
of

my
control
there

is
only
one

way
to
deal

with
what
I

can't
cope
with.

BULLYING

I push
Gemma
into the wall
on the way
to class.

I take
away her chair
in the classroom
so she falls to the floor.

I knock
the sandwich
out of her hand
before she takes a bite.

CAUGHT OUT

I'm shoved
into Mrs Bird's office.

I've had Gemma Griffin's mother in to see me. Do you know why?

She's looking at me
stony-faced.

Do you know WHY?

I'm trying really hard
to be strong,
not weak,
because otherwise I'll cry
and I can't cry.

Look at you. So arrogant.
Gemma's mother has told me
that her daughter has come home crying
every day this week.
How would you like it if someone made you cry?

She's standing right over me.
I can smell her cigarette breath.
I can see the metal fillings
and coffee stains behind her front teeth.

Well? How dare you act so cocky!
Do you want me to call your parents in?

My heart starts beating fast.
She can't call my parents.
Dad will hit Mum,
blame her.

That bitch Gemma Griffin.

She's going to get it for this.
Just because she can't fight back.
Just because she's weak.

I get sent back to art class.
I see her.
I wait.
I stare hard.
She's got no choice.
Her eyes lock with mine
and I mouth,
You fucking wait.

FIRST COMPETITION OF THE SEASON

My legs are like jelly
and I feel sick

        down

            to

                   my

                       toes.

WARM-UPS

Sometimes warm-ups
are more nerve-wracking
than the race.

I focus too much
on the other teams.

I imagine
worst-case scenarios.

FOCUS

Stay in lane.
If you zigzag across,
you're running further and
risk getting tripped up,
or worse,
getting disqualified.

THE RACE 1

I see David on the sideline.
Good luck, he mouths.
I try to focus.

On your marks.

Get set.

Go!

Arms pumping
feet thumping
vision blurred.

I can't quite
catch my breath.

I see Miss Sutton
out of the corner of my eye,
waving her arms.

White lines blur
as my ankle catches
with another runner
and we both
go tumbling
to the ground.

MORTIFIED

On the minibus
back to school,
I'm mortified.
Can't look at anyone,
can't speak to anyone.

It's not the end of the world, Amber.

Miss Sutton being all kind
isn't helping.

How can you say that?
I got disqualified from my first race.

We all make mistakes.
The real test is how you come back from this,
she says.

I see David about to put his hand
on my shoulder and then draw back.

I stare at him.

He looks down.
Guilty.

It feels like my whole world
is crumbling around me.

MAKING AMENDS

David calls to me
as I step off the minibus

I'm sorry, I know I've been off.

Whatever, I don't care.

It's just . . . It's just I'm scared is all.

What have you got to be scared of?

Not me, I'm scared for you.

I should be grateful
but I'm embarrassed.

I'm fine. You don't have to worry.
I'll walk ahead so you don't have to.

Don't push me away.
Don't push Tara away.
We both really care about you.
I just don't know
how to be around you.
I'm so scared for you –
I want to protect you –
but my mum –

Your mum what?

Nothing –
she just said –
you were going to need your friends.
So I'm sorry –
tell me how to be –
tell me what to do –
and I'll do it.

I look into his eyes.
I'd do anything
for one of his
too-tight hugs.

We keep our distance.

I'm sorry,
I say. I'm desperate
to have my friends back.
**Just be you and
I'll be me.**

HARPREET'S WEDDING

A rushed affair
organized in four months.
I hear the talk,
the chatter,
the gossip.

She's learned her lesson. That's for sure.

She's a good girl now.

I'm surprised they managed to find someone willing.
Damaged goods.

At least they chose a good date.
Should bring them good luck.

February 14th.
It couldn't feel less romantic.
I don't think I've seen Harpreet smile
once during the ceremony.
Come to think of it,
I don't think
I've seen her look up.

A NOTE

I write a note for Dad
to give to the boiler man
in the morning.

I tell him I can't stay home from school.
Not any more.

He tries to argue.
I stand my ground.

Just give him this note,
I say.

Dear gasman,

My father doesn't speak English. One of the radiators is leaking. The one
in the small bedroom. The radiators don't get very hot even when the
thermostat is at number 5.
    The boiler sometimes makes a rattling sound when you turn it on. It
lasts about thirty seconds. Lately it's been getting louder.

Please write your findings below and the work you have carried out.

Yours sincerely,

Amber (daughter)

I stick it on the fridge
and go to my room,
shutting the door
on all the name-calling
and swearing
firing at me from the kitchen.

SELF-LEARNING

I'm woken early
by the clink of the tiffin box
and the whistle of the kettle.

As I creep downstairs,
I hear Mum picking out
letters and trying to
sound out words

with the note
for the gasman
in her hand.

A SECOND CHANCE

I hold a bit back,
like ten per cent.

Everyone goes full pelt
at the beginning.

My trick:
save the energy for later.

Give the others some
false hope, then BAM –

last twenty metres
I charge up,

electrify my feet.
My trainers spark

as I gain,
still in lane

and whizzing past.
So fast they don't even see me

cross the finish line
like a firework.

SUCCESS

The county team managers confirm
we've made it
to the second round of the
inter-school competitions.

Singing
and stupid selfies
on the minibus
back home.
Wishing the ride
would last an eternity.

David and I
are as high
as kites.

So high
I don't even
notice we've been
holding hands
the entire
way back to school.

NERVES 1

We walk to our
secret place
in the grounds of
St Martin's.

The air around us
is different.

My legs feel shaky
and my heart is
beating faster than during a
one-hundred-metre sprint.

NERVES 2

You're back.

I never went anywhere.

Yes you did.
Listen, I've wanted to give you something for ages.

He hands me an envelope.
I open it.
Inside is a signed postcard
from Allie Reid!

To Amber
Much love
A. R.

Oh my God!
This is amazing!!

Turn it over.
Read the other side.

You're more than just
my sister from another mister.
You know that, right?

I'm speechless.

Wow, it's really special. You know she's my idol.

Is that all you liked about it?
What about what I wrote?

We're like best mates?

I didn't want to say anything, but Tara said something
about how a life lived with regret is a life half lived or
something, and I just knew that, even if nothing can
happen, you needed to know.

Tara said that?

Yeah, sorry, I had to confide in someone.

I thought you liked Tara.

No. It's always been you.

NERVES 3

We sit,
not talking,
holding hands

for I don't know how long.

Will he
kiss me?
It doesn't

bother me
that I might
be home late.

I don't want
to move
from this spot.

LOVE IS IN THE AIR

I don't feel
my feet touch tarmac
as I float
home.

There is no one
in the house
and I ignore
what the air
around me
already knows.

Because nothing
is going to
take away
this feeling.

TENSION

I listen to Mum
read a picture book.
It's a step up
from the other books.

I help her to
break up words
into smaller chunks
by covering letters
with my thumb.

We hear a key in the lock.
We look at one another –
we weren't expecting him back
this early.

In a panic we throw
the book under the settee.

The door slams,
causing Mum and me
to jump
out of our skin.

SEEN

Mum tries to
calm him down.

I'm running
up the stairs,
need to get into the bedroom –
barricade the door.
A chair,
a washing basket,
stool . . .
sit on the chair,
use your body weight
use your body weight
use your body weight
against Dad pushing on the door.

I've been found out.
Someone spotted me at a competition.
Dad's telling me I've got the devil inside me.
I hear Mum
telling him to calm down,
threatening to call the police.
I'm losing strength.
I can't hold on to the door.
I fall off the chair,
dive on to the bed
and wrap the duvet round me.

Time stops.

HE SAYS

He says   Mum can't help me now.
He says   I should have listened.
He says   I have the devil inside me.
He says   I have to go to the temple.
He says   I have to pray.
He says   I have to pray to get the devil out of me.

TEMPLE

I sit.
I pray.
I pray
for a
way

OUT.

FEAR

Mum tells me to keep
doing what I'm doing.

But fear
follows me into school,
every training session,
every competition.

I keep thinking I see
The Man.

I relive the stories.
I have nightmares.
He haunts
my dreams and
my every waking moment.

CONSUMED

Inflicting pain on others
halves your own hurt
and doubles your
self-worth.

FIGHT BACK

I've got Gemma Griffin cornered
outside the girls' loos.

Why won't you fight back?!

She looks at me,
trying really hard not to cry.
So I punch her,
hard in the stomach.
I've never hit anyone in my life.
It's soft.

She is soft.

FIGHTING BACK

Why are you doing this?
Leave me alone!

She's red-faced.
Standing strong.

This ends.
Now.

She pushes me.
I fall to the floor.

Everyone watching.

Her hand in a fist.
She's still,
heavy-breathing.

Do it, I think.
Do it. Hit me,
so we can be the same.

She picks up her bag.

You're not worth it.

She shoots me one last look
and walks away.

UNDESERVING

Tara and David
are there
with arms
round me
giving me
everything
I don't deserve.

ICELAND LEAFLET

Do you want me to read it for you?
I ask.

Mum says,
No, I want to look at it on my own.
This says . . . best . . . S . . . S . . . guh . . . O . . . What are these words?

Spring Offers. Best Spring Offers.

What is this word?

Chicken.

That's how you spell chicken?

Yes.

And I watch her studying the leaflet.

She looks up.
What? You're thinking I'm stupid?

No!
I'm thinking how proud I am.

MUM

She has fire in her belly.
I think she sees
all she can
become.

DAD'S BACK 4

Turn the volume down,
turn the telly off.

He stands in the doorway,
swaying.

No more.

The last time.

No
more
excuses.

He can wait
five minutes.

When he starts to rage,
I stand in front of Mum.

He tries to take a punch.

I catch his fist.
I hold it tight.

Mum screams.

Leave it. Leave it!
I don't want you to get hurt.

I stand tall.
I stand strong.
My stare unflinching,
my body strong.

And suddenly
Dad doesn't seem
that big any more.

Huh,
I think.

Looks like
I do
have my dad's height
after all.

REBEL

Be a rebel
and rebel.

Be strong
even when you don't feel it.

Scale mountains
even if you're afraid of heights.

They say *don't*,
so you *do*.

They say *can't*,
you say *can*.

Step outside the box.
Colour outside the lines.

Be a rebel
and *rebel*.

SEVEN
OVERTHROW

ANATOMY OF
A REVOLUTION
STAGE 7

Forcible
removal
from
power.

By
any
means
possible.

STANDING STRONG

Dad stumbles
in disbelief.
In shock.

His face
a map of confusion.

We have never
stood up to him before.

He looks smaller,
vulnerable almost.

I want to hug him
and hit him.

I want to say sorry
and scream.

I want to beg for it to stop
so we can stay together,

and I want to run
so we can find a home elsewhere.

I'm still holding his fist when
I push him down on to a chair.

This ends now.

How dare you. How dare you raise your hand to me!

He shakes as the words
leave his mouth.

I'll do whatever it takes to look after Mum.

This isn't you. This isn't my Amber.

It is now.

PACKING OUR BAGS

Mum tells me
we are leaving.

I just need
a small suitcase.

I am to pack the essentials,
we can come back for the rest
another time.

Mum gives me a business card.

Call the number,
she says.

I look at the card.

It's Beena's number.

I was right.
Mum has been thinking
about this for some time.

I want to say no.
I want to say
I stopped him,
I'm stronger now,
I can protect us both.

Why are you hesitating?
Quick, call. We don't have time.

I hear the fear in her voice
and dial Beena's number.

A BARRIER

Dad tries to stop us.
Standing in front of the door.
Blocking our way.

Mum tries to move
him; he grabs her arm.

Stop. Just listen to me.

I pounce.
Let go of her.

I'm still your father.

Then act like one!

We hear a car pull up outside.
Mum looks through the window as
Dad continues to block the door.

LETTING GO

Dad's crying.
He's grabbed hold of Mum's suitcase,
standing in the doorway,
stopping us from leaving.

Why, why, why?

His head in his hands,
pleading.

Mum tells him we're
staying at Ruby's.
Our bags are packed,
Beena is waiting in the car.

His head hung low,
he falls to his knees,
touching Mum's feet,
begging us to stay.

A sight more distressing
than his anger.

We're taking so long,
Beena comes knocking on the door.

Is everything OK?
I hear her shout.

You can leave, this is all your fault.
This is my wife and daughter.
They aren't going anywhere.

Should I call the police?

NO! We'll be OK.

I plead.
Dad, please.
Let us go.
It's just for a night.
We'll be back.
Just let us go.

I don't know if that's true.
I don't know if it's just one night.
I don't know anything right now.

WHAT HAPPENED TO YOU ...

that you can't love?
What happened to you
that evokes so much rage?
What happened to you
that makes you so sad?

I recognize it.
It's inside me,
it's inside Ruby,
it's inside Mum.

An anatomy of sadness.

CHANGE WITHOUT CHANGE

Is there
a way to break free
without breaking us apart?
Is there
a way you can learn from the past
and heal from the hurt?
Is there
a way to stay together
and still move on?
Is there
a way to forgive the person
who has caused you so much pain?

Maybe
if I'm there to defend.
Maybe
now I'm taller and stronger.
Maybe
he'll change and shift into someone else.
Maybe
he'll become the person he was before.

Maybe
we all can.

DRIVING AWAY

Beena takes us to her car.
David is waiting in the back seat.
He gives me a half smile,
a smile desperate to portray
strength and conceal his fear.

I half smile back.
My fear tattooed
on every bit of skin.
I feel completely exposed.

We load our belongings
into the boot.

So strange seeing your life
in a couple of suitcases.

I take one last look at the house.
I see Dad at the kitchen window.

I look across the street.
I see *The Man* outside his house.

He waves at my mother.
I look back at Dad staring out of the window.

I look back at *The Man*.
There's a tightening in my chest

as we drive away from our home
and out of the estate.

THE DRIVE

David shuffles up close
to me in the back seat.
He takes my hand –
I immediately pull away
and mouth,
My mum!

I'm sorry,
he whispers back.
Mum didn't want me to come
but I had to, I couldn't leave you.
Did I do the right thing?

You did.
I'm glad, I say,
but seriously, move over!

This is my son,
Beena tells Mum.

Mum looks at me,
then looks at David
and back at me.

My body, tense
my face, hot
my eyes, failing
to look innocent.

How long will we be gone?

My question remains unanswered
as we drive in silence
to Ruby and Jas's house.

A NEW HOME

Jas pumps air
into blow-up mattresses.

Their lounge
is our bedroom
for the foreseeable future.

I'm trying to take it all in.
Thinking about what this new life means,
what this new life might look like.

There's an unsettled feeling in my gut.
They say Mum is safe now.
But I don't feel safe.
I still feel far from safe.

PANIC ATTACK

It's going
to be
a long
night.

David and I
sit in the kitchen,
helping Jas
cook dinner and
listening to
Ruby and Beena
talking in the lounge.

Beena sits with Mum,
going through options.

I'm not sending them to a refuge,
says Ruby.
They can stay here,
live with us for as long as they want.

Beena talks about
filing charges,
the police,
court injunctions.

Mum's not sure.

I feel
confused.

I always wanted to leave,
but knowing I might
not see him again
makes my heart ache.

You all right, our kid?

Jas takes the garlic
I've been chopping.

I shrug.

**Your mum's really brave.
You're gonna be OK.
You're safe now,**
he says.

There's that word again.
Safe.

You OK, Amber?

David's voice seems distant,
as old fears creep in
and everything starts spinning.

THE LIE

Whoa! you OK?

David's holding my hand
while the room is still spinning and
the smell of burning garlic
makes me want to vomit.

Slowly in . . .
And out . . .
Look at me . . .
In . . . and out . . .

Jas standing over me,
reminding me how to breathe.

You're going to be OK.

Beena, Ruby and Mum
rush into the kitchen.

What's going on?

Mum looks terrified.

She's having a panic attack
but she's OK.

I'm not OK,
I say.
He's going to come after me.

Who?

The Man.

What man?

Everyone but Ruby
seems confused.

David butts in.

**Mr Garcha, who lives across the road.
The one who murdered his daughter . . .**

Mum sits down.
She looks at me.
She seems nervous
and scared,
which makes me
panic again.

**Dad . . . Dad . . . always said . . .
Always said . . . that he'd come for us
if we ever . . . if we ever . . .**

I'm finding it hard
to breathe again.

David puts a hand
on my shoulder,
which instantly calms me.

Mum looks down.

I'm so sorry,
she says.

I'm so sorry.
None of it was true. It was something he said
to keep you from straying . . . I never thought you
would take it seriously, otherwise I never would
have . . . I'm so sorry.

I look at Ruby.

Did you know?

No,
she says, taking a seat.

All this time . . .

FRIENDS

Tara calls.

When she arrives,
we run towards each other
and stay in the tightest hug
for the longest time.

The three of us together.

I know you don't like this sort of stuff,
but here's a crystal. It's got real healing powers.
It's small enough to carry around with you. It works, trust me.

I take the jagged purple stone
and hold it tight in my fist.

Thank you, Tara.

The two of them
breathing courage
and love
into every cell.

Sticking all
the broken pieces
of me

together again.

SLEEPLESS NIGHT

AMBER

My mind is racing.
It won't stop.
I can't make sense of the noise.
I can't separate the images.
I can't hear the words.
It's all so loud,
so confusing,
so heavy.

MUM

I am nobody's property.

Not my husband's.
Not my brother's.
Not my father's.

This I know.

The weight of a wound
carried on my back
for all of my life
slowly lifting.

RUBY

I lie awake,
feeling like a weight
has been lifted,
like a wish
I didn't know I had made
has been granted.

EXTENUATING CIRCUMSTANCES

Ruby comes into school
and talks about my situation
to my head of year.

I hate the looks of sorrow.
I'm strong,
I want to say.
Nothing hurts me,
not any more.

They keep asking if I'm OK
and I keep shrugging.
I don't want to talk.
Why do I need to talk?

I get extenuating circumstances,
which basically means
I can hand work in late.

I'm also told
to go for some counselling.
Which I accept.

Reluctantly.

FAIL

My essay of lies
of a perfect Christmas
failed to impress.

My extenuating circumstances
allow me to resubmit my English essay.

A second chance to pass.
A second chance to

write my truth.

BUNKING OFF SCHOOL

Tara and David
figured I needed a break
from lessons,
from everything.

So are you two together then or what?

With everything that's been happening
I realize I've not spoken to Tara
about David,
the postcard
or anything.

I also realize that
David and I
haven't spoken about
that day either.

What are you guys waiting for?

**I guess we haven't had a chance
to talk about things,**
I say.

Neither of us can look at each other.

Well, don't let me stand in the way. Talk!

Thanks, Tara, but I think we'll talk privately.

*Why? One of you will tell me all the gory
details anyway – this way you save time.*

We sit in silence,
David and I looking
red-faced.

*Ugh! Fine. Have it your way. What do you guys fancy doing?
The world is our oyster!*

I'm happy just hanging out here.

Me too.

Me three.

So that's
exactly
what we do.

NEW ROUTINES

A whole
new way
of life.

A whole
new way
of living.

PARK RUNS

Ruby's house is next to a park.
Living next to green space
is **something** I have always dreamed of.
So now there's no need
to run up and down stairs
for training (I **still** do it sometimes).

I run outside
in the fresh air.
Life **doesn't** get much
better than this.

Jas times my runs
with baby Tiya on his lap.
Sometimes Mum and Ruby
come and watch.
We are starting to **feel**
like a proper family again.

It's everything I ever wanted.
My life feels like
it's on the **right** track.

PLANTING SEEDS

In the school library
I notice a stack of prospectuses
for university.

I use all eight of my tokens
to take them out.

COUNSELLING SESSION 1

I roll my eyes
I sit in silence.
I answer
Yeah
and
No
and occasionally
I shrug my shoulders.

At least I get to miss maths.

IS IT TOO LATE?

I see Gemma
in the hall.
Both of us alone.

I want to talk to her.
I feel nervous and
scared.

I'm scared of *her*.
Her rejection.
She walks past.

I smile,

but she's so used to
looking down,
she doesn't see.

DAD

He's waiting
at the school gates.

He looks thin,
pale
and broken.

I want to run to him.
Beat him and
hold him tight.

David gently holds me back
and Tara stands in front of me.
My human shield.

I see Beena waiting,
watching from the car.

Dad rubs his eyes,
he looks like he's been crying.

I'm going to talk to him.
I'll be OK,
I tell them.

Tara takes my hand.

David and I are going to stand here and watch,
just in case.

I walk towards him.
He seems
so much
smaller now.

Come home,
he croaks.

I can't.

I'm dying.

No you're not.

I am.
Can't you see?
My soul is dying.
Look at me,
look how I shake.

Maybe you should drink less alcohol.

His head hangs low.

Don't come here again.
Mum said I can call the police.
I will next time.

He nods.
Tears fall down his face.
I can smell the alcohol.

I climb into Beena's car
and into David's embrace.
I fight the urge to look back
as we drive off.

CONFLICTED

I feel guilty for not hating him.
I should hate him.

The recipe for hate
has been cooking for years.

Fear, pain, misery, threats, violence, drinking.
What's wrong with me?

No matter how hard I try,
I can't hate him.

I hate myself so easily,
so why isn't it easy to hate him?

I want to hate him,
I really do –
because I should.

A VACANCY

A job
has come up at a supermarket.
They are looking for cleaners.
Mum would earn a proper wage.
No more slave labour.
No more twelve-hour shifts.
No more piecework money.

What do you think?
Should I go for it?

**It's up to you, Mum.
Whatever you want.**

She looks at me
like she's never
had that option
in her whole life.

RUBY HAS TAKEN

notice of the prospectuses
on the coffee table.
She's reading through
them. Dog-earing corners
and making phone calls.
She and Jas look through
the application forms together.

*What do you think?
Should I go for it?*

**Of course you should!
You'll be fighting off offers.**

Ruby looks at Jas
like she's seeing him
for the
first time.

FINALS

We made it to
the regional finals
on 7th May.
It's getting closer,
everyone is holding
their
nerve.

What do you think?
Can I do it?

Yes, Amber, you can.
I support you 100 per cent.

I look at Ruby.
I can't believe what I'm hearing.
We no longer fight, like they fight.
We stand side by side. Finally.

NEW BEGINNINGS

Look at us,
all of us,
flying
into our
futures.

COUNSELLING SESSION 2

It's difficult to start with.
I'm not one for talking.
Sit there in silence
for the first ten minutes.

Awkward.

Tell me what's going on,
she says.

The counsellor
with her
long brown
poker-straight hair
and
gentle face.

Miss Sutton organized all this,
so it doesn't surprise me
she's found someone
with a kind face
like hers.
A face you feel
safe with.

I shrug.

What are you thinking about?

Dunno.
Nothing.
Everything.

Everything?

How long do I have to stay?

This session is an hour,
but you don't have to stay.
You can leave.
Do you want to leave?

I shrug.

Don't know where to start.

There's no rush.

She sits back
in her chair.
We don't talk.
The silence is
suffocating.
The tick of the clock
deafening.

So I let it out.

One

secret

at

a

time.

WHAT I TALK ABOUT

                        Dad
Hate
                                                Love
                Violence
            Hate

Dad
                Ruby
                                                Anger
                        Scared
        Drinking

                                Fear
            The Man
                                        Lies
                        Dreams
                                Mum
        Home
                        Running

                                and Gemma.

                                        Gemma
                                        who
                                        never
                                        deserved
                                        any
                                        of
                                        it.

SECRETS

These secrets
have only ever
been for us.

They were
never meant
to be shared.

Some leap from my mouth
like they've lived forever
on the tip of my tongue
and wished their whole lives
to be freed.

Others are forced
from the pit of my stomach
like splinters living under
layers of skin.
The words bleed
and hurt.

It's hard to admit
what I have borne
witness to.

Even harder
to feel OK about
sharing it.

Even though
I know
deep down
this is
the right thing
to do.

NORMAL

I laugh about *The Man.*
I laugh about the threats of having my bones broken.
I laugh about being told I have the devil inside me.
I laugh about being dragged to the temple.
I laugh
I laugh
I laugh.

The counsellor's eyes widen.
She reins it back.
But I've seen it.

I tell her I'm OK.

I feel it's important
I reassure *her.*

She tells me
it's normal
to try and normalize
my situation.
It's common for people to do this.

But it's not *normal.*

She feels it is important
that she tells *me*
that none of this
is

normal.

RUBY AND MUM

Ruby asks Mum
why it took her so long.

Ruby says,
There are years I can't get back.
A life I could have lived.

Mum says,
I'm sorry.
I didn't know how I could before.

But I begged you.
I begged you.

I know.
Don't you think I remember?
Don't you think I wanted to?

You just didn't care about me.
You wanted me to be as miserable as you.

That's not true.
I didn't know where to go.
We would have been homeless.

You left,
but that doesn't change things for me.
It's still too late for me.

But Jas is a nice man.
He's nothing like your father.

I know he is. But I was eighteen.
I wanted more. I wanted a choice.

JAS

Me, Tiya and Jas
are sitting secretly on the stairs,
listening to the crying
coming from the kitchen.
He puts his head in his hands
and sobs uncontrollably.

A NEW BEDROOM

Mum and I have
taken Tiya's room.

The bed and wardrobe
we ordered from IKEA
have arrived and I spend
the day making furniture
with Jas.

Finally Mum and I
can unpack
our clothes.
No longer living
out of suitcases.

Mum's old workbook
and an old wage packet
fall out of a bundle of clothes.

We stare at it.

So many years,
she says.
So many years.

We sit looking at our
new bedroom,
thinking about our
new future.

A NEW DAY

Me, Jas and Ruby
all wake up early
to see Mum off
on the first day
of her new job.

We watch the sunrise
together,
drinking hot chai.

It's just cleaning.
You didn't have to wake up so early.

Yes we did!
It's a big deal, Mum.
You'll be home in two hours
not twelve!

She smiles.
She knows it is too.
The sun starts to peek
out from behind
the terraced houses.

A new day,
she says.

RUBY AND JAS

Ruby: It's not that I don't love you.

Jas: What then?

We need to start again.

How?

We need to see if we belong together.

What about Tiya?

She's the most important person.

I want to make it work.

I do too.

I'll always support you. You know that, don't you?

I've always known that.

So, let me in.

I'm trying. Give me time.

Have all the time you need. I'm not going anywhere.

COUNSELLING SESSION 3

Trauma can heal.
It's a long journey
but that's what I'm here for.
We'll work through it together,
she says.

Everything you've been feeling,
everything you've done,
it's all connected to your trauma.

Hearing these words
I begin to understand
why.
All the whys.
All the reasons
I am
how I am.

Something starts
to lift
inside me.

STARTING TO UNDERSTAND

I am a bully.
Bullying
made me feel
powerful
in a world
where I felt
worthless.

Dad is a bully.
He must also
feel powerless.

Bullying
comes
from
pain.

You think
inflicting pain
on others
makes your own pain
go away.

It doesn't.

People stay
in bad situations
with bad people
because of fear.

Because they feel
powerless to leave.

Mum felt powerless.
Dad had broken her
down mentally
and physically.

She was broken down
before that
by her own family,
so he had an
easy job.

People think
it's easy to leave.

It isn't.

It's natural to still
love Dad
after everything
he has done.

He's still my dad.
That doesn't
mean it's safe
to stay with him.

Dad needs help.

On some level
Dad is the parent
I think
I deserve
because we're
the same.

We are both
bullies.

I can change.

I want to change.

442

SEEING DAD

I don't know why.
Just seems right.

The house is a mess.
Takeaway trays,
unwashed dishes,
unflushed toilet.

See what becomes of me when you're not here.

You need to learn to take care of yourself.

I think about skipping school,
cleaning the house
and making him a healthy meal.

But it's not my job to fix him.

As I walk out of the estate,
I see Mr Garcha.
I smile, give a little wave.
He smiles,
waves back.

Suddenly there's a release,
a feeling I can't quite describe.

Then it hits me.
I'm not scared.
For the first time,

I feel no fear.

UCAS FORMS

Ruby is applying to university.
Local ones
and ones further away.

**We'll move wherever
she wants to go,**
says Jas.
We'll make it work.

7TH MAY LOOMS

Final training sessions
bringing us
closer together,
making us faster,
stronger,
working as a team.

Final training sessions
bringing David and me
closer together.

Watching each other
on the track,
sitting next to each other
on the bus,
playfully nudging each other
whenever we can.

Which is perhaps
the best thing
of
all.

UNSUCCESSFUL

I try and talk to Gemma.
She doesn't want to know,
and who can blame her?

MACKIE D'S

I try and walk in sight.
I try and own the space around me,
knowing I can be and do
whatever I choose.

There may still be spies
but no one can hurt me.

The impetus to hide behind Tara
is still there.
The need to scan cars
is still there.
Watching out for every auntie
is still there.

Being removed
from a situation
doesn't necessarily
free you from yourself.

7TH MAY

Regional finals.
Miss says the county team managers
are keeping an eye on me.
My times are impressive.
All I have to do is focus.

David and I watch all the other events
like hawks
before it's our time to warm up
for track.

David's up first.

I sit in the stands with
Mum, Tiya, Ruby, Jas, Tara and Beena.
We whoop, shout and cheer as
David runs.
He's like a gazelle,
so swift and strong.

He comes a close second.
I know he'll be disappointed,
but we are so proud.

And now
it's my turn.

I RUN

As I make my way
from the stands,
Tara gives me a hug.

Just be present,
she says.
And everything else will fall into place.

I make my way to the track.
Get into position.
Close my eyes and
take a deep breath.

This is where I belong.

Everything goes quiet.
I look forward.
I hear the gun.
I keep in lane.
I feel the wind.
I hear my breath.
I don't care who's
in front,
to the side
or behind.

I'm not even aware I've won
until I hear my name over the speaker
and see my friends and family
jumping out of their seats.

CHOSEN

I am chosen
straight away
for the county championships

and a second chance
at being the best under-seventeen
two-hundred-metre runner
in the country.

Allie Reid
held this title
when she was my age.

I allow myself to imagine
standing on the podium
holding a gold medal.

For the first time
ever
my dreams seem
possible.

CELEBRATIONS

Mum sits in a restaurant
for the first time.

Have whatever you want,
says Jas.

I sit next to her,
reading the menu,
describing the food,
guessing what she might like.

As we're finishing off our pudding,
we see Dad
shuffling along
the opposite side of the street,
holding a bag
from the off-licence.

I feel guilty
that I don't feel guilty.

I look at Mum.
She's sitting proud,
a defiant look on her face.

She smiles.

Happy?

Yes, Mum. Happy.

WHAT HAPPENED TO DAD?

Orphaned.
Orphanage
abuse.

No love.

No education
no structure
no care
no home.

No love.

Here it was hard.
No friends
no family
no kindness
no belonging.

No love.

When we
came along
he found it
hard to love.

It was
too late
to learn
to love.

CORRECTION

It is

never

too late
to learn
to love.

RUBY'S TRUTH

Ruby's finished her
statement for her university application.
She wants to read it out.

I sit in bed, holding Tiya.
Ready . . .

For my whole life I have always wanted to go to university and study
English. However, it always seemed like a dream. I never thought
someone from my background would have the opportunity to go on
to further education. Over time, my story of being a British Asian girl
hailing from the low-income council estate has grown old; as has my
declaration to become a first-generation university student, building
a legacy for my family.

I can't take my eyes off her.
I listen, holding my breath,
as she reveals all the obstacles
that have held her back.
A marriage she didn't want,
a daughter who came too soon.

My parents, both illiterate in their own language as well as English,
never saw the benefit of education. However, my mother has recently
started learning to read and write, and the change in her view of the
world has been remarkable . . .

She stops.

Is it OK to say all that?

There's a stone in my gut.
These truths have only ever been for us.

Yes.
It's your truth.
Don't be afraid to share it.

My heart is pounding
listening to her read.
Even Tiya is transfixed.

*. . . One day I will change the world. Not only for my younger sister
and my daughter, but for all women. I will lay the foundations, and
I will lead the way.*

I am so proud,
I allow the tears to flow,
bursting with pride.
Tiya bounces up and down.

*Wow-weeee
wow-weeee,
Mummy!*

Did you like Mummy's essay, Tiya?

Wow-weeee, Mummy!

Ruby takes Tiya,
gives her an almighty hug,
lifts her up above her head
making aeroplane noises.
Tiya barely controlling herself
for laughing.

**You're going to fly, Ruby.
I feel it.
You're going to fly!**

PROGRESS

I've been going to counselling
every week
for two months.
I'm showing progress.
My counsellor thinks I'm ready
for the next step.
A step
that will take me out
of my comfort zone.

CHECKING UP

Sometimes
I hang around our old estate
just to catch
a glimpse of him.
Just to see
if he's still alive.

HIDDEN POTENTIAL

Mum's taken
over a sewing class
at the community centre.
Me, Tara and David take part.
We're making tote bags.
I've never seen her interact like this.
She's taking charge,
making jokes,
showing everyone what to do.
She's so
confident.
She's shining in a way
I'd never imagined she could.

COUNSELLING WITH GEMMA

The counsellor thought
it would be a good idea
to have Gemma in the session.

I smile.
Gemma won't look at me.
Who can blame her?

The counsellor asks us questions
and we try and have a conversation,
all three of us.

At one point
Gemma and I

laugh
at the
same thing.

UNIVERSITY

Ruby has been accepted
to a local university.
But it's not her first choice.

Jas has convinced her
to follow her dream,
to set her sights even higher.

In autumn she'll apply to Oxford.
Oxford
is
her
first
choice.

NEW HOME

Mum and I
are rehoused.
It's a small one-bed flat.

Mum makes a small part
of the lounge
into a study area.

A place where we
can read books.

For the first time
since leaving home

I feel
at home.

EIGHT
PEACE

ANATOMY OF
A REVOLUTION
STAGE 8

PEACE.

The war
is over.

A state of normality presides.

However,

inner peace
will take time.

HEADSPACE

I am calmer.
Words flow more easily
now I'm no longer
sitting in a suit of armour.

My hand can't keep up
with the words spilling out
on to the page.

And studying for
exams seems easier
than before.

There is
space in my head
to retain information.

I sit with my English assignment.
My second chance to impress Mr Walker.

I inhale
and
exhale.

It's time
I speak

my truth.

READING

Mum has fallen asleep
with one of Tiya's favourite

picture books in her lap.
I close it carefully so as not to wake her.

I climb into bed
next to her.

I want to feel her warmth.

We did it, Mum.
We did it like
the women in the books,
I whisper.

We rebelled
and we won.

A NEW MUM

I'm learning more
and more about Mum.

Every day she gets
more life in her,
telling stories,
cooking,
sewing.

Stories of childhood.
Family back in India.
And she sings!

I never knew she could.

INNER STRUGGLE

Sometimes
I feel the urge
to relive old feelings,
not because I want to
but because they are familiar.

OLD FEARS

I'm revising for exams.
Tonight it's history.
Revolutions
and their rebels.

It's getting late
and Mum is still not home.
It's 7 p.m.
We would normally start
cooking at this time.

My heart starts racing.
I think of worst-case scenarios.

He's found her.
He's done something.
He said he would.

My eyes start to fill with tears.
I pick up the receiver,
start to dial
999,

when I see it.
A note.

Amber
I gone shop for partee food.
I mite b layte.
No wory.

Mum

PROUD

I give her the biggest hug
before she's even through the door.

Your note was brilliant! I'm so proud.

Did I write it all correctly?

Yes,
I lie.

Without thinking
I start to read the receipt out loud.

You don't need to do that any more,
she says.
I know what I bought.

HOUSE-WARMING

There has never
been music,
dancing,
laughing,
singing,
or colours
in my home
before.

I savour
every moment.

THE BOY

So this boy . . .
Mum asks.

She continues clearing
the table of plastic cups and plates.

You like this boy?

I shrug my shoulders.
I feel nervous and sick.
Familiar fears,
never too far from the surface,
come simmering up.

My body feels weak.
I nearly drop a plate of
leftover party food
on the way to the kitchen.

You can tell me.

I don't know if I can.
I don't know if this is still
the one area of our lives
where we will always hold
different views.

But I'm tired of keeping things hidden.
I want to live a full life.
I take a deep breath.

Yes,
I say nervously.

OK. That's OK,
she says.

Just be careful. He looks like a heartbreaker.

She pauses.

But then it's better to love and feel heartbreak,
no matter how many times, than never having loved at all.

LONDON!

I've made it to the ESAC
county championships.
I'm in London
a day early
as a treat.

The school team
has come along to
support me.

David and I can't believe
how crazy London is.

We're walking slow,
wanting to take it all in,
and everyone is tutting around us,
rolling their eyes.

I keep getting shoved on the escalator
for not standing on the right side.

At lunch we go into Mackie D's
because it's all we can afford.
After lunch we go down to
Carnaby Street in Soho.
It's the coolest place in London
after Oxford Street.
The shops are more expensive
and there are loads of people
sitting outside cafes drinking frothy coffee
and whipped-cream hot chocolates
and bubble teas.
I spot a shop with a name I recognize.

Sarah knows it too,
but not like I do.

Oh my God. I LOVE their jeans.
They fit so well. Can we go in, Miss?

My heart races as we go In.

I look at the price tag.
One hundred and twenty pounds.
My mum used to get
two pounds an hour
to dye them
and Sarah pays
one hundred and twenty pounds
to wear them.

FIRST KISS

David and I
split from the group to
take a moment alone
in Hyde Park.

I'm so proud of you.

Thanks.

Not just for making it to the county championships,
for everything. You've been through so much.
I think you're amazing.

He takes my hands
in his hands.
My heart, racing.
My breath, held,
as his lips
touch mine
for the first time.
Right there
on a bridge
over a lake
in Hyde Park.

I'm
in
heaven.

BREATHING

I feel like I can breathe.
Like my lungs
have filled
themselves up
to the brim
for the first time.
I realize
I've only ever
been half breathing.

THE RACE 2

On your marks . . .

Feet on the blocks.

Get set . . .

Focus.

Wait for the sound of the gun . . .

. . . and I'm off!

Accelerating,
arms pumping,
legs driving
me forward

into
my future and
towards
my dreams.

DEAR MR WALKER

I write now
what I could not
before.

My truth.

Here
it
is.

All the secrets
I've been holding inside
about dreams so big
and love so grand,
a life half lived.

About Mum,
about Ruby,
about Dad,

about me.

How we fought,
how we survived,
how we rebelled.

I write it all.

Here.

I am no longer
bound by secrets,
silenced by fear.

This is the truth.
I own it and
it is mine to tell.

EPILOGUE

I am   reborn.

I am   strength.
I am   power.
I am   warmth.
I am   soft.
I am   rough.
I am   diamond.
I am   tiger.
I am   courage.
I am   healed.
I am   leader.
I am   revolution.
I am   rebellion.

I am   Amber Rai

and

I am   *REBEL.*

AUTHOR Q&A

WHAT INSPIRED YOU TO WRITE RUN, REBEL?

Like all writers, I draw upon many things including my own experience. Essentially, I wanted to write for my teenage self – the teenager who felt quite isolated and voiceless, and therefore, the adult me is passionate about empowering women and girls any way I can.

This passion inspired the creation of Run The World, an organization that works with women and girls from marginalized backgrounds and helps to empower them through sport and storytelling. It's been really inspiring seeing the women I work with grow stronger and more confident with each running session, and hearing their brave, life-changing stories. It gave me the confidence to dig deep and share an untold story, which I believe will resonate with many people, through Amber's voice in *Run, Rebel*.

WHY DID YOU CHOOSE TO WRITE A NOVEL IN VERSE?

I find writing in verse quite liberating. It was easier to deal with big emotional subjects by getting straight to the heart of the issue and saying more with very little. I also like playing with structure, and I like how verse novels can bring words to life on a page with the use of white space and by playing with key phrases. It forces you to want to speak the words out loud, which I think appeals to the actress in me.

DO YOU HAVE A FAVOURITE CHARACTER IN THE STORY?

That's a difficult one to answer but if I have to pick one character, I think it's Mum. The courage it takes her to follow through every act of rebellion cannot be underestimated. She's a real warrior. For me, she goes on the biggest journey in the book. I also have a soft spot for Tara. She's really wise and she's a great friend. We'd all be really lucky to have a Tara in our lives.

WHY DID YOU DECIDE TO MAKE AMBER A RUNNER? WHAT DOES RUNNING MEAN TO YOU?

Running has always been a big part of my life. It encourages positive mental health by reducing stress and anxiety. That's the main reason I made Amber a runner. I knew her character needed an outlet for her sadness and anger (which is usually sadness in disguise). I really believe that all sports, not just running, have the capacity to empower and impact change, and I wanted to explore that impact through Amber's character.

WERE THERE ANY PARTS OF THIS NOVEL THAT WERE DIFFICULT TO WRITE?

Weirdly the happy, lighter bits. The darker more emotional topics came quite easily. (I'm not too sure what that says about me.) The earlier drafts of the novel were quite dark, and I was told I needed to balance that out. What's perhaps more troubling is that I didn't see those early drafts as particularly dark. Looking back, I can see that they were, so it's been a real learning curve . . . and not just for my writing!

WHAT WOULD YOU LIKE READERS TO TAKE AWAY FROM THIS STORY?

Hope and resilience. No matter how impossible something may seem, there is always a way out.

ARE THERE ANY OTHER BOOKS THAT YOU'D RECOMMEND FOR FANS OF *RUN, REBEL*?

Definitely: *I am Thunder* by Muhammad Khan, *The Hate You Give* by Angie Thomas, *The Poet X* by Elizabeth Acevedo. They all feature strong, inspiring and complex heroines, and are therefore particular favourites of mine.

DO YOU HAVE ANY ADVICE FOR ASPIRING AUTHORS?

If you have an idea, start it, be consistent and focus. Turn up and write. It doesn't have to be every day – you might not have that luxury – but do you have thirty minutes once a week? Writing is just about turning up when you promised yourself you would and focusing. Don't worry about being perfect. Just get your story down on paper.

ACKNOWLEDGEMENTS

Thank you to the women who dared to try something new, who put on a pair of trainers and walked, jogged or ran with me every week. To those women who grew in confidence with every stride. To those women who dared to challenge, make a stand and refused to accept less. To those women who encouraged each other, shared their stories and supported one another. You are the bravest and most brilliant women I know. You are the true rebels.

Thank you to my brilliant editor Carmen McCullough. You immediately grasped what I was trying to do, and your unwavering enthusiasm and kindness throughout the entire process supported me through some difficult stretches. You really are quite wonderful, and I am so thankful *Run, Rebel* found its way to you.

Thank you to Alice Sutherland-Hawes, my amazing agent. Your instant belief and championing of the book gave me hope and belief in myself. You are nothing but supportive, and I am so grateful that we found each other.

Thank you to the fabulous Penguin WriteNow team, especially Ruth Knowles who saw something in my first few thousand words and carried the unfinished manuscript forward. I will never forget our first meeting in Birmingham. Your words of encouragement made me feel like I belonged in the world of publishing, a defining moment and turning point in my life. Thank you to Siena Parker who works tirelessly on delivering the WriteNow programme and supporting all of us mentees. To the inaugural

WriteNow family: here's to your continued success. A special thank-you to Emma Smith-Barton, Nazneen Ahmed and Katie Hale. You three supported me so effortlessly in times of need, and for that I will be forever grateful.

Where would I be without all the fabulous people who worked on *Run, Rebel*. A book is a collaboration, and I couldn't be more grateful to the following collaborators who helped *Run, Rebel* shine in a way I could never have done alone: the wonderful Amelia Lean, copy-editor extraordinaire Shreeta Shah, you are one in a million, and Jane Tait, thank you so much for your insight. Thank you to the fabulous proofreaders Toria Chilvers, Sarah Hall and Pippa Durn – what you do is nothing short of incredible. A massive thank-you to Emily Smyth and Janene Spencer who worked tirelessly on design and fonts – I know how difficult it was, and I appreciate your care and dedication. Also, a huge thank-you to Manjit Thapp for her beautiful cover art. Michelle Nathan and Simon Armstrong, I am so thankful for your marketing and PR brilliance. I must also add Wendy Shakespeare to this list. Your advice and understanding helped alleviate my (often) panicked state, and I will always be grateful for the hand-delivered proofs! A special thank-you to the audiobook team: James Keyte, without whom it wouldn't have happened; Roy McMillan who directed and created a wonderful audio recording and provided me with the most fun two days in the studio; and the amazing audiobook editor Daniel Murguialday. I am so grateful to you all and consider myself very lucky to have been in the care of such wonderful folk.

I cannot begin to express my gratitude at being awarded The John C Laurence Award from the Authors' Foundation. Finding the time and space to write is extremely challenging. This award not only allowed me the valuable time to finish the novel, but knowing there were others who believed in my work was a huge confidence boost and support in getting this book finished. I will forever be grateful.

Thank you to my cheerleaders: Sandy Sidhu and Leeanna Elliot – almost three decades of friendship – I would be completely lost without you both. Sarah Foster, my earth angel, Sue Harrison, my inspiration, and Sadie Hurley, I would not have made it through to the end of this book without our sea-swimming and coffee mornings. You are the best friends a woman could ask for. Your consistent support means everything to me. And of course, my Joey. I write because you encouraged me to, and I continue because you won't let me quit! Thank you. Thank you for believing in me more than I believe in myself. You lovely bunch of humans are my family.

ABOUT THE AUTHOR

Manjeet is an actress, playwright,
screenwriter and director. She is the
founder of Run The World – an organization
that works with women and girls from
marginalized backgrounds and helps to
empower them through sport and
storytelling. She lives in Kent.